13.95

INTERIM SITE

3 1192 00403 3542

JL 1983

L'Engle, Madeleine

And both were young

EVANSTON PUBLIC LIBRARY
CHILDREN'S DEPARTMENT
1703 ORRINGTON AVENUE
EVANSTON, ILLINOIS 60201

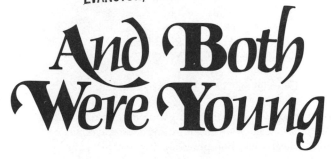

And Both Were Young

MADELEINE L'ENGLE

℗ DELACORTE PRESS / NEW YORK

Published by
Delacorte Press
1 Dag Hammarskjold Plaza
New York, N.Y. 10017

Copyright © 1983 by Crosswicks, Ltd.

All rights reserved. No part of this book may be reproduced
or transmitted in any form or by any means, electronic
or mechanical, including photocopying, recording, or by
any information storage and retrieval system, without the
written permission of the Publisher, except where
permitted by law.

Manufactured in the United States of America

First printing

Library of Congress Cataloging in Publication Data
L'Engle, Madeleine.
And both were young.
Summary: Philippa is miserable at an all girls' boarding
school in Switzerland until she forms a supportive
friendship with the mysterious Paul.
[1. Boarding schools—Fiction. 2. School stories.
3. Friendship—Fiction.] I. Title.
PZ7.L5385Am   1983   [Fic]   82–72751
ISBN 0–440–00264–8

FOREWORD

When *And Both Were Young* was first published, there were a great many very simple things that could not be put in a book that was to be read by children and young adults. Death, for instance: it was assumed that children should be protected from death, and that they should not, in fact, know that death exists. And sex: of course parents produced children in some airy, unphysical fashion. So I had to tone down the effect of Philippa's mother's death, and the interest of other women in her father. And Philippa's and Paul's mutual attraction.

So the portions that are now in the book that were not in the original are truer to the original typescript than what was actually printed. I have changed only to restore, for this book was written a long time ago, when I was a very young woman, and I've grown a lot, and learned a lot, and all of this change is reflected in what I write now.

Philippa's experiences are very similar to my own boarding school experiences. And I have become a professional writer, so I know that she has become a professional artist, because a portrait by Philippa Hunter is important in my new novel, *A Severed Wasp*.

To Jo

I saw two beings in the hues of youth
Standing upon a hill, a gentle hill . . .
And both were young—and one was beautiful
Lord Byron,
The Dream, Canto II

CONTENTS

ONE
The Prisoner of Chillon

"Where are you going, Philippa?" Mrs. Jackman asked sharply as Flip turned away from the group of tourists standing about in the cold hall of the château of Chillon.

"I'm going for a walk," Flip said.

Her father put his hand on her shoulder. "I'd rather you stayed with us, Flip."

She looked up at him, her eyes bright with pleading. "*Please*, father!" she whispered. Then she turned and ran out of the château, away from the dark, prisoning stones and out into the sunlight that was as bright and as sudden as bugles. She ran down a small path that led to Lake Geneva, and because she was blinded by sudden tears and by the sunlight striking on the lake she did not see the boy or the dog sitting on a rock at the lake's edge, and she crashed into them.

"I'm sorry!" she gasped as the boy slid off the rock and one of his legs went knee-deep into the water before he was able to regain his balance. She looked at his angry, handsome face and said quickly, this time in French, "I'm terribly sorry. I didn't see you."

"You should watch where you're going!" the boy cried and bent down to wring the water out of his trouser leg. The dog, a large and ferocious brindle bull, began leaping up at Flip, threatening to knock her down.

"Oh—" she gasped. "Please—please—"

"Down, Ariel. Down!" the boy commanded, and the bulldog dropped to his feet and then lay down in the path in front of Flip, his stump of a tail wagging with such frenzy that his whole body quivered.

The boy looked at Flip's navy blue coat. "I'm afraid Ariel got your coat dirty. His paws are always muddy."

"That's all right," Flip said. "If I let it dry, it will brush off." She looked up at the boy standing very straight and tall, one foot on the rock. Flip was tall ("I do hope you won't grow any *taller*, Philippa dear," Mrs. Jackman kept saying), but this boy was even taller than she was and perhaps a year older.

"I'm sorry I knocked you into the lake," Flip said.

"Oh, that's all right. I'll dry off." The boy smiled; Flip had not realized how somber his face was until he smiled. "Is anything the matter?" he asked.

Flip brushed her hand across her eyes and smiled back. "No. I was just—in a rage. I always cry when I'm mad. It's terrible!" She blew her nose furiously.

The boy laughed. "May I ask you a question?" he said. "It's to settle a kind of bet." He reached down and took hold of the bulldog's collar, forcing him to rise to his feet. "Now sit properly, Ariel," he commanded, and the dog dropped obediently to its haunches, its tongue hanging out as it panted heavily. "And try not to drool, Ariel," the boy said. Then he smiled at Flip again. "You *are* staying at the Montreux Palace, aren't you?"

"Yes." Flip nodded. "We came in from Paris last night."

"Are you Norwegian?"

"No. I'm American."

"She was right then," the boy said.

"Right? About what? Who?" Flip asked. She sat down on the rock at the edge of the water and Ariel inched over until he could rest his head on her knee.

"My mother. We play a game whenever we're in hotels, my parents and I. We look at all the people in the dining room and decide what nationalities they are. It's lots of fun. My mother thought you were American, but my father and I thought maybe you were Norwegian, because of your hair, you know."

Flip reached up and felt her hair. It was the color of very pale corn and she wore it cut quite short, parted on the side with a bang falling over her rather high forehead. Mrs. Jackman had suggested that she have a permanent, but for once Flip's father had not agreed. "She has enough wave of her own and it suits her face this way," he said, and Mrs. Jackman relented.

"Your hair's very pretty," the boy said quickly. "And it made me wonder if you mightn't be Scandinavian. Your father's so very fair too. But my mother said that your mother couldn't be anything but American. She said that only an American could wear clothes like that. She's very beautiful, your mother."

"She isn't my mother," Flip said. "My mother is dead."

"Oh." The boy dropped his eyes. "I'm sorry."

"Mrs. Jackman came from Paris with Father and me." Flip's voice was as hard and sharp as the stone she had picked up and was holding between her fingers. "You'd have thought she was just waiting for mother to die, the way she moved in."

"Was your mother ill long?" the boy asked.

"She was killed in an automobile accident. A year ago. She's always being terribly kind, Mrs. Jackman, I mean, and doing things for me, but I think she doesn't care if I live or die. What I think is, she lusts after my father." Now the words were muffled. She had never said this before. She had thought it, but she had not said it.

"I'm sorry," the boy said again, then, as though to cut the tension, "Watch out that Ariel doesn't drool on your skirt," he said. "One of his worst faults is drooling. What's your name?"

"Philippa Hunter. What's yours?" She tried to relax.

"Paul Laurens. People—" he hesitated, "people who aren't your own parents can sometimes be wonderful. I know—" He broke off as though he had said too much.

"Not Mrs. Jackman," Flip said.

"She's very beautiful."

"Beauty is only skin deep, according to my grandmother. And Eunice's skin may not be thick, but it's not deep either. She makes me call her Eunice, and I hate that. We're not friends. And when she calls my father 'darling' I want to hit her. She's the one I got so mad at just now, so I knocked you into the lake." She looked at Paul in apology and surprise. "I've never talked about Eunice before. Not to anyone."

"Well," Paul said, "sometimes you get to a point where you have to spill things out, or you burst."

"I guess I was there," Philippa said. "Thanks for not being put off."

"Don't be silly. And it's safe with me. Ariel's made your coat very dirty. I hope it will brush off. You have on a uniform, don't you?"

"Yes," Flip answered, and her voice was harsh again because tears were threatening her again. "I'm being sent to boarding school, and it's all because of Eunice Jackman wanting me out of the way so she can get her claws into Father. He'd never have thought of making me go away to school if Eunice hadn't persuaded him it was—what did she say?—inappropriate—for me to travel around with him while he makes sketches for a book."

"That's too bad. But—well, my mother has to be travelling all winter. She's a singer, and she's going to be on tour. So Father and I are managing alone."

"But you'll be with your father," Flip said. She looked out across the lake, forcing the tears back.

"What do you want to do when you get out of school?" Paul asked.

"Be an artist, like Father. School won't help me to be an artist." She continued to stare out over the water, and her eyes rested on a small lake steamer, clean and white, passing by. "I should like to get on that boat," she said, "and just ride and ride forever and ever."

"But the boat comes to shore and everybody has to get off at last," Paul told her.

"Why?" Flip asked. "Why?" She looked longingly after the boat for a moment and then she looked at the mountains that seemed to be climbing up into the sky. They looked like the mountains that she imagined when she looked up at cloud formations during the long, slow summers in Connecticut. Now she was in Switzerland

and these were real mountains, with real snow on their
dazzling peaks. "Well—" she stood up, dislodging Ariel.
"I'd better go back now. Eunice Jackman will think I'm
off weeping somewhere. She says Mother's been dead
nearly a year and I should stop moping. She's doing her
best to stop Father moping, that's for sure." Now that she
had started talking about Eunice, it seemed she could not
stop. "She's already had two or three husbands, and she
wants to add Father to her collection. If I'm in boarding
school I can't stop her. I don't know what's the matter
with me, going on this way. I'm sorry, Paul."

"It's all right." Paul took her hand. His grip was firm
and strong. "Ariel doesn't usually take to people the way
he's taken to you. When Ariel doesn't like people I
know I'm never going to like them, either. He has very
good taste. Perhaps we'll meet again sometime. I'd like
that."

"I'd like it, too." Philippa returned his smile. "It doesn't
sound likely, with me being incarcerated in boarding
school."

"I'm sorry about that," Paul said. "It sounds awful. I
hate institutions. But Switzerland's a small country, and
my father and I are going to spend the winter up on the
mountain while Mother's on tour. She goes tomorrow.
They've been wandering around the château this morning; they love it. It's where my father proposed to my
mother." He smiled again and then his face changed and
became so serious that Flip looked at him in surprise. "I
don't like it, because I don't like any place that's been a
prison." But then his face lightened and he said, "Do you
know that poem of the English poet, Byron? *The Prisoner
of Chillon?* It's about a man who was a prisoner in the
château."

"Yes," Flip said. "We studied it in English last year. I didn't like it much, but I think I shall pretend that my school is a prison and I am the prisoner and at Christmas my father will rescue me."

"If he doesn't," Paul said, "I will."

"Thank you," Flip said. "Are you—do you go to school?"

The same odd, strained look came into Paul's eyes that had darkened them when he mentioned prisons. "No," he said. "I'm not going to school right now."

"Well . . . good-bye," Flip said.

"Good-bye." Paul shook hands with her again. She turned clumsily and patted Ariel's head; then she started back up the path toward the château of Chillon.

About halfway to the château she saw her father coming down the path toward her. He was alone, so she ran up to him and caught hold of his hand.

"All right now, Flippet?" Philip Hunter asked.

"Yes, father."

"It's not as though it were forever, funny face."

"I know, father. It's all right. I'm going to pretend that the school is the château of Chillon and I'm the prisoner, and then at Christmas you'll come and liberate me."

"I certainly will," Philip Hunter said. "Now let's go find Eunice. She's worried about you."

Eunice Jackman was waiting for them, her hands plunged into the pockets of her white linen suit. Her very black hair was pulled back from her face into a smooth doughnut at the nape of her neck. "Only a very beautiful woman should wear her hair like that," Philip

Hunter had told Flip. Now he waved at Eunice and shouted, "Hi!"

"Hi!" Eunice called, taking one hand leisurely out of her pocket and waving back. "Feeling better, Philippa?"

"I can't feel better if I haven't been feeling badly," Flip said icily. "I just wanted to go for a walk."

Eunice laughed. She laughed a great deal, but her laugh never sounded to Flip as though she thought anything was funny. "So you went for a walk. Didn't you like the château, Philippa?" Eunice never called her Flip.

"I don't like to look at things with a lot of other people," Flip said. "I like to look at them by myself. Anyhow, I like the lake better. The lake and the mountains."

Mrs. Jackman looked over at Philip Hunter and raised her eyebrows. Then she slipped her hand through his arm. Flip looked at him, too, at the short straw-colored hair and the intense blue eyes, and her heart ached with longing and love because she was to be sent away from him.

"Wait till you get up to the school," Mrs. Jackman said. "According to my friend, Mrs. Downs, there's a beautiful view of the lake from every window. You're going to adore school once you're there, Philippa."

"Necessities are necessary, but it isn't necessary to adore them," Flip said. She hated herself for sounding so surly, but when she was with Mrs. Jackman she always seemed to say the wrong things. She stared out over the lake to the mountains of France. She wanted to go and press her burning cheeks against the cool white-ness of the snowy tips.

"Well, if you're determined to be unhappy, you probably will be," Mrs. Jackman said. "Come on, Phil," and

she patted Philip Hunter's arm. "It's time to drive back
to the hotel and have lunch, and then it will be time to
take Philippa up to the school. Most girls would con-
sider themselves extremely fortunate to be able to go
to school in Switzerland. How on earth did you get so
dirty, Philippa? You're all covered with mud. For heav-
en's sake, brush her coat off, Phil. We don't want her
arriving at the school looking like a ragamuffin."

Flip said nothing. She reached for her father's hand
and they walked back to the tram that would take them
along the lake to the Montreux Palace.

While they were washing up for lunch Flip said to her
father, "Why did she have to come?"

"Eunice?"

"Yes. Why did she have to come?"

Philip Hunter was sitting on the edge of the bed, his
sketch pad on his knee. While Flip was drying her hands
he was sketching her. She was used to being sketched at
any and all odd moments and paid no attention. "Father," she prodded him.

At last he looked up from the pad. "She didn't have to
come. She offered to come since it was she who suggested this school, and it was most kind of her. You're
very rude to Eunice, Flippet, and I don't like it."

"I'm sorry," she said, leaning against him and looking
down at the dozens of little sketches on the open page of
his big pad. She looked at the sketch he had just finished
of her, at the quick line drawings of people in the tram,
of Eunice in the tram, of sightseers in the château, of
Eunice in the château, of Eunice drinking coffee in the
salon of the Montreux Palace, of Eunice on the train
from Paris, of Eunice sitting on a suitcase in the Gâre
Saint-Lazare. She handed the pad back to him and went

over to her suitcase filled with all the regulation blouses and underclothes and stockings Eunice had bought for her; it was so very kind of Eunice. "I don't see why I can't stay with you," Flip said.

Philip Hunter got up from the bed and took her hands in his. "Philippa, listen to me. No, don't pull away. Stand still and listen. I should have left you in New York with your grandmother. But I listened to you and we did have a beautiful summer together in Paris, didn't we?"

"Oh, yes!"

"And now I suppose I should really send you back to New York to Gram, but I think you need to be more with young people, and it would mean that we couldn't be together at Christmas, or at Easter. So in sending you to school I'm doing the best I can to keep us together as much as possible. I'm going to be wandering around under all sorts of conditions making sketches for Roger's book, and you couldn't possibly come with me even if it weren't for missing a year of school. Now be sensible, Flip, please, darling, and don't make it harder for yourself and for me than it already is. Eunice is right. If you set your mind on being unhappy, you will be unhappy."

"I haven't set my mind on being unhappy," Flip said. "I don't want to be unhappy."

"Everything's understood then, Flippet?"

"I guess so."

"Come along down to the dining room then. Eunice will be wondering what on earth's keeping us."

After lunch, which Flip could not eat, they took her to the station. Flip's ticket said: *No. 09717 Pensionnat*

Abelard—Jaman—Chemin de Fer Montreux Oberland Bernois Troisième Classe, Montreux à Jaman, valable 10 jours. Eunice was very much impressed because there were special tickets for the school.

The train went up the mountain like a snake. The mountain was so steep that the train climbed in a continuous series of hairpin bends, stopping frequently at the small villages that clustered up the mountainside. Flip sat next to the window and stared out with a set face. Sometimes they could see the old gray stones of a village church, or a glimpse of a square with a fountain in the center. They passed new and ugly stucco villas occasionally, but mostly old brown chalets with flowers in the windows. Sometimes in the fields by the chalets there would be cows, though most of the cows were grazing farther up the mountain. The fields and roadsides were full of autumn flowers and everything was still a rich summer green. At one stop there was a family of children, all in blue denim shorts and white shirts, three girls and two boys, waiting for the pleasant-looking woman in a tweed suit who stepped off the train. All the children rushed at her, shouting, "Mother! Mother!"

"Americans," Eunice said. "There's quite a considerable English and American colony here, I believe."

Flip stared longingly out the window as the children and their mother went running and laughing up the hill. She thought perhaps Paul and his mother were happy in the same way. She felt her father's hand on her knee and she said quickly, "Write me lots, father. Lots and lots and lots."

"Lots and lots and lots," he promised as the train started again. "And the time will pass quickly, you'll

see. There's an art studio where you can draw and paint.
You'll be learning all the time."

Eunice lit a cigarette although there was a sign saying
NO SMOKING in French, Italian, and German. All the
notices were in French, Italian, and German. DO NOT
SPIT. DO NOT LEAN OUT THE WINDOW. DO NOT PUT BAGS
OUT THE WINDOW. "The next stop's Jaman," Eunice said.

Something turned over in Flip's stomach. I should be
ashamed, she thought. I should be ashamed to be so
scared.

But she was scared. She had never been separated,
even for a night, from her entire family. During the war
when her father had been in Europe, her mother was
still alive; and then in the dark days after her mother's
death Gram had come to live with them; and afterward,
whenever her father had to go away for a few days
without her, at least Gram had been there. Now she
would be completely on her own. She remembered her
mother shaking her once, and laughing at her, and saying, "Darling, darling, you must learn to be more inde-
pendent, to stand on your own feet. You must *not* cling
so to Father and me. Suppose something should happen
to us? What would you do?" That thought was so pre-
posterously horrible that Flip could not face it. She had
flung her arms around her mother and hidden her head.

Now she could not press her face under her mother's
arm and escape from the world. Now she was older,
much older, almost an adult, and she had to stand on
her own feet and not be afraid of other girls. She had
always been afraid of other girls. In the day school she
went to in New York she had long intimate conversations with them all in her imagination, but never in re-
ality. During recess she sat in a corner and drank her

chocolate milk through a straw and read a book, and whenever they had to choose partners for anything she was always paired off with Betty Buck, the other unpopular girl. And on Tuesdays and Thursdays when they had gym in the afternoon, whenever they chose teams Flip was always the last one chosen; Betty Buck could run fast so she was always chosen early. Flip couldn't run fast. She had a stiff knee from the bad time when her kneecap had been broken, so it wasn't entirely her fault, but that didn't make it any easier.

However, in New York, Flip didn't mind too much about school. She usually finished her homework in her free period, so when she got home the rest of the day was hers. If her father was painting in his studio, she would sit and watch him, munching one of the apples he always kept in a big bowl on the table with his jars of brushes. Sometimes she cleaned his brushes for him and put them back carefully in the right jars, the blue ginger jar, the huge green pickle jar, the two brass vases he had brought from China. Flip loved to watch him paint. He painted all sorts of things. He painted a great many children's portraits. He had painted literally dozens of portraits of Flip, and one of them was in the Metropolitan Museum of Art, and people had bought some of the others. It always seemed strange to Flip that people should want a picture of someone else's child in their homes.

Sometimes Philip Hunter did illustrations for children's books and Flip had all of these books on her bookshelves; it seemed that she could never outgrow them. They were in the place of honor, and whenever she was sick in bed or unhappy she would take them out and look at them. The book he was doing illustrations for now was one which he said was going to be very beautiful and important, and it was a history of lost children all through the ages. There would be pictures of the lost children in the children's crusade and the lost children in the southern states after the civil war and in Russia after the revolution, and now he was going to travel all around drawing pictures of lost children all over Europe and Asia, and he told Flip that he hoped maybe the book would help people to realize that all these children had to be found and taken care of.

When Flip thought about all the lost children she felt a deep shame inside herself for her anger and resentment against Eunice and for the hollow feeling inside her stomach now as the train crawled higher and higher up the mountain. She was not a lost child. She would have a place to eat and sleep and keep warm all winter, and at Christmastime she would be with her father again.

Now the train was slowing down. Eunice stood up and brushed imaginary specks off her immaculate white skirt. Philip Hunter took Flip's suitcase off the rack. "This is it, Flippet," he said.

An old black taxi took them farther up the mountain to the school. The school had once been a big resort hotel and it was an imposing building with innumerable red-roofed turrets flying small flags, and iron balconies were under every window. The taxi driver took Flip's bag and led them into a huge lounge with a marble floor and stained glass in the windows. There should have been potted palms by the marble pillars, but there weren't. Girls of all ages and sizes were running about, reading notices on the big bulletin board, carrying suitcases, tennis racquets, ice skates, hockey sticks, skis, cricket bats, lacrosse sticks, armfuls of books. A wide

marble staircase curved down into the center of the hall.
To one side of it was a big cagelike elevator with a sign,
FACULTY ONLY, in English, French, German, Italian,
and Spanish. At the other side of the staircase was what
had once been the concierge's desk with innumerable
cubbyholes for mail behind it. A woman with very dark
hair and bushy eyebrows sat at it now, and she looked
over at Eunice and Flip and Philip Hunter inquiringly.
They crossed the hall to the desk.

"This is Philippa Hunter, one of the new girls,"
Eunice said, pushing Flip forward. "I am Mrs. Jackman
and this is Mr. Hunter."

The black-haired woman behind the desk nodded and
reached for a big notebook. Flip noticed that she had
quite a dark mustache on her upper lip. "How do you
do? I am Miss Tulip, the matron," she said as she began
leafing through the ledger. "Hartung, Havre, Hesse,
Hunter. Ah, yes, Philippa Hunter, number ninety-seven,
room thirty-three." She looked up from the book and
her black eyes searched the girls milling about in the big
hall. "Erna Weber," she called.

A girl about Flip's age detached herself from a cluster
and came over to the desk. "Yes, Miss Tulip?"

"This is Philippa Hunter," Miss Tulip said. "She is in
your dormitory. Take her upstairs with you and show
her where to put her things. She is number ninety-seven."

"Yes, Miss Tulip." Erna reached down for Flip's suitcase and a lock of fair hair escaped from her barrette
and fell over one eye. She pushed it back impatiently.
"Come on," she told Flip.

Flip looked despairingly at her father, but all he did
was to grin encouragingly. She followed Erna reluctantly.

At the head of the stairs Erna set down the suitcase

and undid her barrette, yanking her short hair back tightly from her face. *"Sprechen Sie deutsch?"* she asked Flip.

Flip knew just enough German to answer *"Nein."*

"Parlez-vous français?" Erna asked, picking up the suitcase again.

To this Flip was able to answer *"Oui."*

"Well, that's something at any rate," Erna told her in French, climbing another flight of marble stairs. "After prayers tonight we aren't supposed to speak anything but French. Some of the girls don't speak any French when they first come and I can tell you they have an awful time. I ought to know, because I didn't speak any French when I came last year. What did Tulip say your name was?"

"Philippa Hunter."

"What are you? English?"

"No. American."

Erna turned down a corridor, pushed open a white door marked 33, and set the suitcase inside. Flip looked around a sunny room with flowered wallpaper and four brass beds. Four white bureaus beside the beds and four white chairs at the feet completed the furnishings. Wide French windows opened onto a balcony from which Flip could see the promised view of the lake and the mountains. Each chair had a number painted on it in small blue letters. Erna picked up the suitcase again and dumped it down on the chair marked 97.

"That's you," she said. "You'd better remember your number. We do everything by numbers. That was Miss Tulip at the desk; she's the matron and she lives on this floor. We call her 'Black and Midnight.' She's a regular old devil about giving order marks. If one corner of the bed isn't tucked in just so or if you don't straighten it the minute you get off it or if a shirt is even crooked in a drawer, old Black and Midnight gives you an order mark. So watch out for her. Have you got any skis?"

Flip nodded. "They were sent on with my trunk."

"Oh. They'll be in the ski room then. Rack ninety-seven. Your hook in the cloak room will be ninety-seven too." Erna pulled open one of the drawers in Flip's bureau. "I see you sent your trunk in time. Black and Midnight's unpacked for you."

"That was nice of her," Flip said.

"Nice? Don't be a child. They unpack for us to make sure there isn't any candy or money or food in the trunks, or books we aren't supposed to read, or lipstick or cigarettes. Have you got anything to eat in your suitcase?"

Flip shook her whirling head.

"Oh, well, you'll learn," Erna said. "Come on. I'll find your cubicle in the bathroom for you and we'll see what your bath nights are. Then I'll take you back down to Miss Tulip. I suppose you want to say good-bye to your mother and father."

Flip started to explain that Eunice wasn't her mother, but Erna was already dragging her down the hall. "*Himmel*, you're slow," Erna said. "Hurry up."

Flip tried to stumble along faster with her long legs. Her legs were very long and straight and skinny, but sometimes it seemed as though she must be bowlegged, knock-kneed, and pigeon-toed all at once, the way she always managed to stumble and trip herself up.

Erna pushed open a heavy door. Down one side of the wall were rows and rows of small cubicles, each marked with a number. Each had a shelf for a toothbrush, mug, and soap, and hooks underneath for towels. On the opposite wall were twelve cubicles, each with a wash basin, and a curtain to afford a measure of privacy. "'The johns are next door," Erna said. "Here's the bath list. Let's see. You're eight forty-five Tuesday, Thursday, and Saturday. That's my time too. We can bang on the partition. Once Black and Midnight found a girl crawling under the partition and she was expelled."

Erna's French was fluent, with just a trace of German in it. Flip had learned to speak excellent French that summer in Paris, so she had no difficulty in following it, though she herself had nothing to say. But Erna seemed to be perfectly happy dominating the conversation.

"Come on," Erna said. "I'll take you downstairs, and you can say good-bye to your parents. I want to see if Jackie's come in from Paris yet. She's one of our roommates. This is her third year here."

"Jackie what?" Flip asked, for something to say.

"Jacqueline Bernstein. Her father directs movies. Last year he came over to see Jackie and he brought a movie projector with him and we all had movies in Assembly Hall. It was wonderful."

They had reached the big entry hall now and Flip looked around but could not see either her father or Eunice, and at this point even Eunice would have been a welcome face. Erna led her up to the concierge's desk where Miss Tulip still presided.

"Well, Erna, what is it now?" the matron asked.

"Please, Miss Tulip," Erna said, her hands clasped meekly in front of her. "You said I was to show this new girl our room and everything, so I did."

Miss Tulip looked at Erna, then at Flip, then at her notebook. "Oh, yes. Philippa Hunter, number ninety-seven. Please take her to Mademoiselle Dragonet, Erna. Her father is waiting there for her."

"Come on," Erna told Flip impatiently.

Mlle. Dragonet's rooms were at the end of the long corridor on the second floor and were shut off from the rest of the school by heavy sliding doors. These were open now and Erna pulled Flip into a small hall with two doors on each side. She pointed a solemn finger at the first door on the right. "This is the Dragon's study," she said. "Look out anytime you're sent there. It means you're in for it." Then she pointed to the second door. "This one's her living room and that's not so bad. If you're sent to the living room, you're not going to get a lecture, anyhow, though the less I see of the Dragon the happier I am."

"Is she?" Flip asked.

"Is she what?"

"A dragon."

"Old Dragonet? Oh, she's all right. Kind of stand-offish. Doesn't fraternize much, if you know what I mean. But she's all right. Well, I've got to leave you now, but I'll see you later. You just knock."

And Flip was left standing in the empty corridor in front of the Dragon's door. She gave a final despairing glance at Erna's blue skirt disappearing around the curve of the stairs. Then she lifted her hand to knock because if her father was in there she didn't know how else to get to him. Besides, she didn't know what else to do. Erna had deserted her, and she would never have the courage to go back to the big crowded lounge or to try to find her room again all alone. She tapped very gently, so gently that there was no response. She hugged herself in lonely misery. Oh, please, she thought, please, God, make me not be such a coward. It's awful to be such a coward. Mother always laughed at me and scolded me because I was such a coward. Please give me some gumption, quick, God, please.

Then she raised her hand and knocked. Mlle. Dragonet's voice called, "Come in."

The rest of the day had the strange, turbulent, uncontrolled quality of a dream. Flip said good-bye to her father and Eunice in Mlle. Dragonet's office, and then she was swept along in a stream of girls through registration, signing up for courses, dinner, prayers, a meeting of the new girls in the common room . . . she thought that now she knew what the most unimportant little fish in a school of fishes must feel like caught in the current of a wild river. She sat that night on her bed, her long legs looking longer than ever in candy-striped pajamas, and watched her roommates. On the bureau beside the bed she had the package her father had left her as a going-away present: sketch pads of various sizes and a box of Eberhard Faber drawing pencils. There was also a bottle of Chanel No. 5 from Eunice, which she had pushed aside.

"You'll have to take those downstairs tomorrow morning," Erna told her. "We aren't allowed things like that in our rooms. You can put it in your locker in the common room or on your shelf in the classroom. They'll be marked with your number."

Flip felt that if she heard anything else about her number, she would scream. She was accustomed to being a person, not a number, and she didn't like number 97 at all. But she just said, "Oh."

Jacqueline Bernstein, the other old girl in the room, pulled blue silk pajamas over her head and laughed. Flip had noticed that she laughed a great deal, not a giggle, but a nice laugh that bubbled out of her at the slightest excuse, like a small fountain. She was a very pretty girl with curly black hair that fell to her shoulders and was held back from her face with a blue ribbon the color of her uniform, and she had big black eyes with long curly lashes. Her body had filled out into far more rounded and mature lines than Flip's. "Remember when old Black and Midnight caught me using cold cream last winter?" she asked Erna. "She'll let you use all kinds of guk like mentholatum on your face to keep from getting chapped, but not cold cream because it's makeup."

Flip looked at her enviously, thinking disparagingly of her own sand-colored hair and her eyes that were neither blue nor gray and her body as long and skinny as a string bean. That's just it, she thought. I look like a string bean and Jacqueline Bernstein looks like somebody who's going to be a movie star and Erna looks like somebody who always gets chosen first when people choose teams.

She hoped her grandmother was right when she said she would grow up to be a beauty, but when she looked at Jackie, Flip doubted it.

The door opened and Gloria Browne, the other roommate, came in. She was English, with ginger-colored permanent-waved hair. Erna had somehow discovered and informed Flip and Jackie that Gloria's parents were tremendously wealthy and she had come to school with four brand new trunks full of clothes and had two dozen of everything, even toothbrushes. "Esmée Bodet says Gloria's *nouveau riche*," Erna added. "Her father owns a brewery and an uncle in Canada or someplace sent her the clothes."

"Esmée always finds out everything about everybody," Jackie had said. "I don't know how she does it. She's an awful snoop."

Now Gloria walked to her bureau and took up her comb and started combing out her tangles.

"Use a brush," Erna suggested.

"Oh, I never use a brush, ducky," Gloria said. "It's bad for a permanent."

Jackie laughed. "That's silly."

"Your hair's natural, isn't it?" Gloria asked.

"But yes."

"Have you ever had a permanent?"

"No."

"Then don't say it's silly. If you brush a permanent, all the wave comes out."

Jackie laughed again and got into bed. "Well, at least you speak French," she said. "At least we won't have to go through *that* struggle with you."

"Oh, I went to a French school in Vevey before the war." Gloria gave up on her tangles. "This is my fifth boarding school. I started when I was six."

"How are you at hockey?" Erna asked.

Gloria shrugged and said, "Oh, not too bad," in a way that made Flip know she was probably very good indeed.

"How about you, Philippa?" Erna asked.

Flip admitted, "I'm not very good. I fall over my feet."

"How about skiing?"

Gloria pulled a nightgown made of pink satin and

ecru lace over her head. "I just dote on skiing. We spent last Christmas hols at St. Moritz."

"I've never skied," Flip said, "but everybody says I'm going to love it."

Erna looked at Gloria's nightgown. "If you think Black and Midnight's going to let you wear that creation, you're crazy."

Jackie looked at it longingly. "It's divine. It's absolutely divine."

Gloria giggled. "Oh, I know they won't let me wear it. I just thought I'd wait till they made me take it off. Emile gave it to me for a going-away present."

"Who's Emile?" Erna asked.

"My mother's fiancé. He's a count."

"A count—pfft!" Jackie laughed.

"He is too. And he has lots of money, which most counts don't nowadays."

"Your mother's *what?*" Erna asked.

"Her fiancé. You know. The man she's going to marry. Emile is a card. And he gives me wonderful presents. And then Daddy gives me presents so I won't like Emile better than I do him. It really works out very well. I'm just crazy about Emile. Daddy likes him too."

"Your *father!*" Jackie squeaked.

"Oh, yes. Mummy and Daddy are still great friends. Mummy says it's the way civilized people behave. She and Daddy both hate scenes. Me too."

"But don't you just feel awful about it?" Erna asked.

"Awful? Why? I don't expect it'll make much difference to me. I'll spend the summer hols with Mummy one year and with Daddy the next, and as soon as I'm out of school I expect I'll get married myself unless I decide to have a career. I might get Emile to give me a dress shop in London or Paris. I expect he would and I adore being around pretty frocks and things. Isn't it a bore we have to wear beastly old uniforms here? We didn't have uniforms at my last school, but there were vile ones the school before."

A bell rang, blaring so loudly that Flip almost fell off the bed. She didn't think she'd ever be able to hear that bell without jumping. It rang for all the classes, Erna had told her, and in the evenings it rang at half hour intervals, announcing the times at which the different age groups were to put out their lights. For meals one of the maids got in the elevator with a big gong and rode up and down, up and down, beating the gong. Flip liked the gong; it had a beautiful resonant tone, and long after the maid had stopped beating it and left the elevator you could hear the waves of rich sound still throbbing through the building, and with closed eyes you could almost pretend it was a jungle instead of a school.

"That's our bell," Erna said. "Black and Midnight comes in to put out the light. That's one trouble with being on this floor. She gets to us so soon."

As she finished speaking the door was opened abruptly and Miss Tulip stood looking in at them. She had changed to her white matron's uniform. "Everybody ready?" she asked.

Erna and Jackie chorused, "Yes, Miss Tulip, thank you, Miss Tulip."

Then Miss Tulip spotted Gloria's nightgown. "Really!" she exclaimed. "Gloria Browne, isn't it?"

Gloria echoed Erna and Jackie. "Yes, Miss Tulip, thank you, Miss Tulip."

"That nightgown is most unsuitable," Miss Tulip said disapprovingly. "I trust you have something else more appropriate."

"That depends on what you call appropriate, please, Miss Tulip," Gloria said.

"I will go over your things tomorrow. Report to me after breakfast."

"Yes, Miss Tulip," Gloria said meekly, and winked at Erna.

"Good night, girls. Remember, no talking." And Miss Tulip switched out the light.

Flip lay there in the dark. As her eyes became accustomed to the night she noticed that the lights from the terrace below shone up through the iron railing of the balcony and lay in a delicate pattern on the ceiling. She raised herself on one elbow and she could see out of the window. All down the mountainside to the lake the lights of the villages lay like fallen stars. As she watched, one would flicker out here, another there. Through the open window she could hear the chime of a village church, and then, almost like an echo, the bell from another church and then another. She began to feel the sense of wonderful elation that always came to her when beauty took hold of her and made her forget her fears. Now she saw the lights of the train as it crawled up the mountain, looking like a little luminous dragon. And on the lake was a tiny band of lights from one of the lake boats.

Oh, beautiful, beautiful, beautiful! she thought. Then she began to long for her father to show the beauty to. She couldn't contain so much beauty just in herself. It had to be shared, and she couldn't whisper to the girls in her room to come and look. She couldn't cry, "Oh,

Erna, Jackie, Gloria, come look!" Erna and Jackie must know how beautiful it was, and somehow Flip thought that Gloria would think looking at views was stupid. Father, she thought. Oh, father. What's the matter with me? What is it?

Then she realized. Of course. She was homesick. Every bone in her ached with homesickness, as though she were getting the flu. Only she wasn't homesick for a place, but for a person, for her father. How many months, how many weeks, how many days, hours, minutes, seconds, till Christmas?

She sat in the warm tub on her first bath night and longing for her father overflowed her again and she wept. Miss Tulip entered briskly without knocking.

"Homesick, Philippa?" she asked cheerfully. "I expect you are. We all are at first. But you'll get over it. We all do. But you mustn't cry, you know! It doesn't help. Not a bit. Sportsmanship, remember."

Flip nodded and watched the water as it lapped about her thin knees.

"Almost through?"

"Yes."

"Yes, Miss Tulip," the matron corrected her.

"Yes, Miss Tulip," Flip echoed obediently.

"Well, hurry up then. It's almost time for the next girl. Mustn't get a tardy mark by taking more than your fifteen minutes."

"I'll hurry," Flip said.

"Washed behind your ears?"

"Yes." Flip was outraged that Miss Tulip should ask

her such a question. But Miss Tulip with another brisk nod bounced out as cheerfully as she had entered. Flip stepped out of the tub and started to dry herself.

They were supposed to start hockey, but it rained, and Flip's class had relay races in the big gym at the other end of the playing fields from the school. The gym had once been the hotel garage, but now it was full of bars and rings and leather horses and an indoor basketball court where the class above Flip's was playing. Erna and a Norwegian girl, Solvei Krogstad, were captains. Erna chose Jackie, then dutifully chose Gloria and Flip. It was to be a simple relay race. The girls were to run with a small stick to the foot of the gym and back, putting the stick into the hand of the next girl. Flip was fifth in line, following Gloria.

Gloria ran like a streak of lightning. Sally Buckman, the girl behind Flip, was jumping up and down, shrieking, "Keep it up, Glory! Oh, Glory, swell!"

Gloria snapped the stick smartly into Flip's fingers, but Flip fumbled and dropped it. Sally groaned. Flip picked up the stick and started to run. She ran as fast as she could. But her knee seemed stiffer than it ever had before and her legs were so long that she had no control of them and her feet kept getting in their own way. She heard the girls screaming, "Run, Philippa, *run*, can't you!" Now she had reached the end of the gym and she turned around and started the long way back to Sally Buckman. The girls were jumping up and down in agony and their shouts were angry and despairing. "Oh, Philippa! Oh, Philippa, *run!*"

Panting, her throat dry and aching, she thrust the stick into Sally's hand and limped to the back of the line.

After gym she locked herself in the bathroom and again read the letter from her father which had come in the morning mail. It was a gay, funny letter, full of little sketches. She answered it during study hall, hoping that the teacher in charge would not notice. She drew him a funny picture of Miss Tulip, and little sketches of her roommates and some of the other girls. She told him that the food wasn't very good. Too many boiled potatoes. And the bread was doughy and you could almost use it for modeling clay. But maybe it would help her get fat. She did not tell him that she was homesick and miserable. She could not make him unhappy by letting him know what a terrible coward she was. She looked around at the other girls in the study hall, Sally chewing her pencil, Esmée twisting a strand of hair around and around her finger, Gloria muttering Latin verbs under her breath.

Gloria had whispered to her that the teacher taking study hall was the art teacher. Her name was Madame Perceval, and she was Mlle. Dragonet's niece. The girls called her Percy, and although she had a reputation for being strict, she was very popular. Flip stared at her surreptitiously, hoping that she wouldn't be as dull and unsympathetic as the art teacher in her school in New York. She had finished her lessons early and now that she had written her letter to her father she did not know what to do. She thought that Madame Perceval looked younger and somehow more alive than the other teachers. "I wonder where her husband is?" Gloria had whispered. "Jackie says nobody knows, not even Esmée. She

says everybody thinks there's some sort of mystery
about Percy. I say, isn't it glamorous! I can't wait for the
first art lesson."

Madame Perceval had thick brown hair, the color of
well-polished mahogany. It was curly and quite short
and brushed back carelessly from her face. Her skin was
burnished, as though she spent a great deal of time out
of doors, and her eyes were gray with golden specks.
Flip noticed that study hall tonight was much quieter
than it had been the other nights with other teachers in
charge.

She reached for a pencil to make a sketch of Madame
Perceval to put in the letter to her father and knocked
her history book off the corner of her desk. It fell with a
bang and she felt everybody's eyes on her. She bent
down to pick it up. When she put it back on her desk she
looked at Madame Perceval, but the teacher was writing
quietly in a notebook. Flip sighed and looked around.
There was no clock in study hall and she wondered how
much longer before the bell. Erna, sitting next to her at
the desk by the window, was evidently wondering the
same thing, because Flip felt a nudge; she looked over,
then quickly took the rolled-up note Erna was handing
to her. She read it. "How many more dreary minutes?"

Flip reached across the aisle and nudged Solvei Krogstad, who had a watch. Solvei took the note, looked at
her watch, scribbled "ten" on the note, and was about to
pass it back to Flip when Madame Perceval's voice
came clear and commanding.

"Bring that note to me, please, Solvei." Flip was very
thankful that she wasn't the one who had been caught.

Solvei rose and walked up the aisle to the platform
on which the teacher's desk stood. She handed the note

to Madame Perceval and waited. Madame Perceval looked at the note, then at her own watch.

"Your watch is fast, Solvei," she said with a twinkle. "There are fifteen more dreary minutes, not ten."

Very seriously Solvei set her watch while everybody in the room laughed.

After study hall, while they were all gathered in the common room during the short period of free time before the bell that sent them up to bed, Gloria said to Flip, "I say, that was decent of Percy, wasn't it?"

Flip nodded.

"Imagine Percy being the Dragon's niece!" Then Gloria yawned. "I say, Philippa, have you any brothers or sisters?"

Flip shook her head.

"Neither have I. Mummy and Daddy didn't really want me, but I popped up. Accidents will happen, you know. They said they were really glad, and I'm not much trouble after all, always off at school and things. In a way I'm rather glad they didn't want me, because it relieves me of responsibility, doesn't it? I always have enough responsibility at school without getting involved in it at home."

Erna and Jackie wandered over. "Hello. What are you two talking about?"

"Oh, you," Gloria said.

Erna grinned. "What were you saying?"

"Oh, just how lucky we were to get you two as room-mates."

Erna and Jackie looked pleased, while Flip stared at Gloria in amazement.

"Are you ever called Phil, Philippa?" Erna asked suddenly.

Flip shook her head. "At home I'm called Flip."

Jackie laughed and Erna said, "Flip, huh? I never heard of anyone being called a name like Flip before."

Gloria began to giggle. "I know what! We can call her Pill!"

Jackie and Erna shouted with laughter. "Pill! Pill!" they cried with joy.

Flip did not say anything. She knew that the thing to do was to laugh, too, but instead she was afraid she might burst into tears.

"Let's play Ping-Pong before the bell rings," Jackie suggested.

"Coming, Pill?" Gloria cried.

Flip shook her head. "No, thank you."

She wandered over to one of the long windows and stepped out onto the balcony. The wind was cool and comforting to her hot cheeks. The sky was full of stars and she looked up at them and tried to feel their cold clear light on her upturned face. Across the lake the mountains of France loomed darkly, suddenly breaking into brightness as the starlight fell on their snowy tips. Flip tried to imagine what it would be like when all the mountains and valleys were covered with snow.

From the room behind her she could hear all the various evening noises, the sound of the phonograph playing popular records, the click, click, click of the Ping-Pong ball Erna, Jackie, and Gloria were sending over the net, and the excited buzz of general conversation. Although the girls were supposed to speak French at all times, this final period of freedom was not supervised, and Flip heard snatches of various languages, and of the truly international language the girls had developed, a potpourri of all their tongues.

"Ach," she heard someone saying, "I left *mein cein-
ture dans le* shower *ce morgen. Quelle* dope *ich bin!"*

She sat down on the cold stone floor of the balcony
and leaned her face against the black iron rail. The rail
felt cold and rough to her cheek. She looked down to the
path below where Miss Tulip in her white uniform was
walking briskly between the plane trees. Flip sat very
still, fearful lest the matron look up and see her.

The bell rang. Out here on the balcony it did not
sound so loud. She heard the girls in her class putting
books, records, and note paper into their lockers and
slamming the doors, and she knew that she would have
to come in and follow them upstairs. But not yet. Not
quite yet. It would take them a little while to get everything put away. She heard someone else walking along
the path below and looked down and recognized Madame Perceval. Madame Perceval stopped just below
Flip's balcony and leaned against one of the plane trees.
She stood there very quietly, looking down over the lake.

She thinks it's beautiful, too, Flip thought, and suddenly felt happier. She scrambled to her feet and went
back into the common room just as Gloria and a group
of girls were leaving. They saw her.

"Oh, here comes Pill!" Gloria shouted.

"Hello, Pill!" they all cried.

The brief happiness faded from Flip's eyes.

Almost the most difficult thing, Flip found, was never
being alone. From the moment she woke up in the morning until she fell asleep at night, she was surrounded by
girls. She was constantly with them, but she never felt
that she was of them. She tried to talk and laugh, to be

like them, to join in their endless conversations about boys and holidays, and clothes and boys, and growing up and again boys, but always it seemed that she grew clumsier than ever and the wrong words tumbled out of her mouth. She felt like the ugly sister in the fairy tale she had loved when she was younger, the sister whose words turned into hideous toads, and all the other girls were like the beautiful sister whose words became pieces of gold. And she would stand on the hockey field when they chose teams, looking down at her toe scrounging into the grass, and pretend that she didn't care when the team that had the bad luck to get her let out a groan, or the gym teacher, Fraülein Hauser, snapped, "Philippa Hunter! How can you be so clumsy!" And Miss Tulip glossed over Jackie's untidy drawers and chided Flip because her comb and brush were out of line. And Miss Armstrong, the science teacher, cried, "Really, Philippa, can't you enter the classroom without knocking over a chair?" And when she fell and skinned her knees Miss Tulip was angry with her for tearing her stockings and even seemed to begrudge the iodine that she put on Flip's gory wounds.

If only I knew a lot of boys and could talk about them, she thought, or if I was good at sports.

But she had never really known any boys, and sports were a nightmare to her.

So in the common room she stood awkwardly about and tried to pretend she liked the loud jazz records Esmée played constantly on the phonograph. Usually she ended up out on the balcony, where she could at least see the mountains and the lake, but soon it became too cold out on the balcony in the dark, windy night air and she was forced to look for another refuge. If she

went to the empty classroom, someone always came in
to get something from a desk or the cupboard. They
were not allowed to be in their rooms except at bedtime
or when they were changing for dinner or during the
Sunday afternoon quiet period. She was lonely, but
never alone, and she felt that in order to preserve any
sense of her own identity, to continue to believe in the
importance of Philippa Hunter, human being, she must
find, for at least a few minutes a day, the peace of
solitude. At last, when she knew ultimately and forever
how the caged animals constantly stared at in the zoo
must feel, she discovered the chapel.

The chapel was in the basement of the school, with
the ski room, the coat rooms, and the trunk rooms. It
was a bare place with rough white walls and rows of
folding chairs, a harmonium, and a small altar on a
raised platform at one end. Every evening after dinner
the girls marched from the dining room down the stairs
to the basement and into the chapel, where one of the
teachers read the evening service. Usually Flip simply
sat with the others, not listening, not hearing anything
but the subdued rustlings and whisperings about her. But
one evening Madame Perceval took the service, reading
in her sensitive contralto voice, and Flip found herself
listening for the first time to the beauty of the words:
"Make a joyful noise unto the Lord, all the earth: make
a loud noise, and rejoice, and sing praise. Sing unto the
Lord with the harp, and the voice of a psalm . . . let the
hills be joyful together." And Flip could feel all about
her in the night the mountains reaching gladly toward
the sky, and the sound of the wind on the white peaks
must be their song of praise. The others, too, as always
when Madame Perceval was in charge, were quieter, not

more subdued but suddenly more real; when Flip looked at them they seemed more like fellow creatures and less like alien beings to fear and hate.

After chapel that evening, when they were back in the common room, Flip pretended that she had left her handkerchief and slipped downstairs again to the cold basement. She was afraid of the dark, but she walked slowly down the cold corridor, lit only by a dim bulb at the far end, blundering into the trunk room, filled with the huge and terrifying shapes of trunks and suitcases, before she opened the door to the chapel.

Down one wall of the chapel were windows, and through these moonlight fell, somehow changing and distorting the rows of chairs, the altar, the reading stand. Flip drew in her breath in alarm as she looked at the organ and saw someone seated at it, crouched over the keys. But it was neither a murderer lying in wait for her nor a ghost, but a shadow cast by the moon. She slipped in and sat down on one of the chairs and she was trembling, but after a while her heart began beating normally and the room looked familiar again.

She remembered when she was a small girl, before her mother died, she had had an Irish nurse who often took her into the church just around the corner from their apartment. It was a small church, full of reds and blues and golds and the smell of incense. Once her nurse had taken her to a service and Flip had been wildly elated by it, by the singing of the choirboys, the chanting of the priest, the ringing of the bells; all had conspired to give her a sense of soaring happiness. It was the same kind of happiness that she felt when she saw the moonlight on the mountain peaks or the whole Rhone valley below her covered with clouds, and she could lean out over the balcony and be surrounded by cloud, lost in cloud, with only a branch of elm appearing with shy abruptness as the mist was torn apart.

Here in the nondenominational chapel at school she felt no sense of joy; there was no overwhelming beauty here between these stark walls, but gradually she began to relax. There was no sound but the wind in the trees; she could almost forget the life of the school going on above her. She did not try to pray, but she let the quiet sink into her, and when at last she rose she felt more complete; she felt that she could go upstairs and remain Philippa Hunter who was going to be an artist, and she would not be ashamed to be Philippa Hunter, no matter what the girls in her class thought of her.

At last she rose and started out of the chapel, bumping into a row of chairs with a tremendous clatter. The noise shattered her peace and she stopped stock still, her heart beating violently, but when nothing else happened, when no one came running to see who had desecrated the chapel, she walked swiftly out on tiptoe. She opened the door and came face-to-face in the corridor with Miss Tulip in her stiff white matron's uniform.

"Well! Philippa Hunter!"

Flip felt as though she had been caught in some hideous crime. She looked wildly around.

"Where have you been?" Miss Tulip asked.

"In the chapel—" she whispered.

"Why?" Miss Tulip snapped on her pince-nez and looked at Flip as though she were some strange animal.

Flip could not raise her voice from a stifled whisper. "I wanted to—to be alone."

Miss Tulip looked at Flip more curiously than ever. "That's very nice, I'm sure, Philippa, dear, but you must remember that there is a time and place for everything. You are not allowed in the chapel except during services."

"I'm sorry," Flip whispered. "I didn't know." She looked away from Miss Tulip's dark frizzy hair and down at her feet. It seemed that she had seen more of feet since she had been at school than in the rest of her life put together.

"We won't say anything about it this time." Miss Tulip looked at Flip's bowed head. "Your part's not quite straight, Philippa. It slants. See that you get it right tomorrow."

"Yes, Miss Tulip."

"Now run along and join the other girls. It's nearly time for lights-out."

"Yes, Miss Tulip." Flip fled from the matron and the musty dampness of the corridor.

But she knew that she would go back to the chapel.

The following day art was the last class of the morning. Madame Perceval had said to the new girls, "I want you to paint me a picture. Just anything you feel like. Then I will know more what each one of you can do."

Flip was painting a picture of the way she thought it must look up on the very top of the snow-tipped mountains, all blues and lavenders and strange misshapen shadows. And there was a group of ice children in her picture, cold and wild and beautiful. During the first art class they had just drawn with pencil. Now they were using water color.

Madame Perceval came over and looked at Flip's picture. She stood behind Flip, one strong hand resting lightly on her shoulder, and looked. She looked for much longer than she had looked at anyone else's picture. Flip waited, dipping her brush slowly in and out of her cup of water. Finally Madame said, "Go on and let's see what you're going to do with it." She didn't offer suggestions or corrections as she had with most of the others, and as she moved on to the next girl she pressed Flip's shoulder in a friendly fashion.

The art studio was on the top floor of the building. It was a long white room with a skylight. There were several white plaster Greek heads, a white plaster hand, a foot, and a skull, and in one corner a complete skeleton which was used only by the senior girls in advanced art. The room smelled something like Flip's father's studio and the minute Flip stepped into it she loved it and she knew that Madame Perceval was a teacher from whom she could learn. She chewed the end of her brush and thought fiercely about her painting and her ice children and then twirled her brush carefully over the cake of purple paint. Now she had completely forgotten the school and being laughed at and her incompetence on the playing fields and being screamed at and left out and pushed away. She was living with her ice children in the cold and beautiful snow on top of the mountain, as silver and distant as the mountains of the moon.

She did not hear the bell and it was a shock when Madame Perceval laughed and said, "All right, Philippa. That's enough for this time," and she saw that the others had put their paints away and were hurrying toward the door.

There was almost fifteen minutes before lunch and Flip knew that she could not go to the classroom or the common room without losing the happiness that the art lesson had given her. She wanted to go someplace quiet, where she could read again the letter from her father that had come that morning. She thought of the chapel and she thought of Miss Tulip. It's Miss Tulip or God, she said to herself, and went to the chapel.

In the daylight there were no moving shadows; everything was as white and clean as the snow on the mountain peaks. Flip sat down and read her letter, warmed by its warmth. She was once again Philippa Hunter, a person of some importance, if only because she was important to her father and he had taught her to believe that every human being was a person of importance. After she had finished the letter for the third time she put it back in her blazer pocket and sat there quietly, thinking about the picture she had been painting that morning, planning new pictures, until the bell rang. Then she hurried up the stairs and got in line with the others.

Because she was the tallest girl in the class she was last in line, but Gloria twisted around from the middle of the row calling, "I say, Pill, where did you rush off to after art?"

"Oh—nowhere," Flip said vaguely.

"Nowhere! You must have been somewhere!" Gloria cried. "Come on, Pill, where were you?"

Flip knew that Gloria would persist until she had found out, so she answered in a low voice, "In the chapel."

"The chapel!" Gloria screeched. "What were you doing in the chapel!"

"You mean you went there when you didn't *have* to go?" Erna asked. Flip nodded.

"What for?"

"Pill, are you nuts?"

They were all looking at her as though she were crazy and laughing at her.

Oh, *please*, she thought. I can't even go to chapel to be quiet without its being something wrong.

Kaatje van Leyden, one of the senior prefects responsible for keeping order, called out, "Quiet!" and the chattering subsided.

But she knew that that would not be the end of it.

Gloria said one morning as they were making their beds and Erna and Jackie had not yet come up from breakfast, "I say, Philippa, you don't mind my saying something, do you, ducky?"

"What?" Flip asked starkly.

"I mean because of us both being new girls and everything, I thought I ought to tell you."

"What?" Flip asked again.

"Well, Pill, if I were you I wouldn't keep running off to chapel, that's all."

Flip smoothed out her bottom sheet and tucked it in. "Why not?"

"The kids think it's sort of funny."

"I know they do." Flip pulled up her blankets and straightened them out.

"How do you know?" Gloria asked.

Flip's voice was tight. "I'm not deaf. Anyhow, I heard you laughing in the common room with them about it."

"I never did."

"I heard you."

"You eavesdropped."

"I didn't. I walked into the common room and I couldn't help hearing. Anyhow, I don't go running off to chapel. I just go there once in a while. There's nothing wrong with that."

"You know, Pill," Gloria said, cocking her head and looking at Flip curiously, "somehow I never thought of you as being particularly pious."

Flip looked startled. "I don't think I am. I mean, I never thought about it."

"Then what do you go running off to chapel for? Don't you go there to pray or something?"

"No," Flip said. "At least I usually do say a prayer or something, because if I go there I think it's only courteous to God. But I really go there to be alone."

"To be alone?"

"Yes. There isn't any other place to go."

"What do you want to be alone for?" Gloria asked.

"I just do," Flip said. "If you don't know why, I can't explain it to you, Gloria."

"You're a funny kid, Pill," Gloria said. "You'd be all right if you just gave yourself a chance."

Jackie and Erna came in then and Gloria turned back to making her bed.

Jackie pulled Flip aside one evening after chapel. They waited until everyone had gone into the common room, then Jackie pulled Flip into the dining room. The maids had finished clearing away the dinner dishes and the tables were already set for breakfast the next morning. Jackie seemed embarrassed and unhappy.

"Philippa, I want to say something to you." They stood under the long box of napkin racks, each little cubbyhole marked with the inevitable number. Flip stared at Jackie and waited. Jackie looked away, looked up over Flip's head, over the napkin racks, up to the ceiling. "I want to apologize to you."

"What for?" Flip asked.

"My mother said I should apologize to you," Jackie said rapidly, still looking up at the ceiling, her hands plunged deep into the pockets of her blue blazer, "about our laughing about your going to chapel. I always write my mother everything and I wrote her about our thinking it was funny and laughing and she wrote back and said who am I of all people to laugh. She said if you got down on the floor in the middle of the common room and bowed toward Mecca I should honor and respect your form of worship."

"Oh," Flip said. She felt that she ought to try to explain to Jackie that it really wasn't a burning question of religion that led her to brave Miss Tulip's annoyance and go to the chapel, but she was afraid that Jackie would not understand and might even be angry.

Jackie had finished her uncomfortable quoting from her mother's letter and she looked down at her feet. "So I do apologize," she said. "I'm very sorry, Pill."

"That's all right," Flip answered, embarrassed, but making an effort to sound friendly.

Jackie heaved a sigh of relief. "Well, I've got to go now," she almost shouted. "The others are waiting for me." She tore off and Flip was left standing under the napkin racks.

Saturday afternoons they had free time. Most of the girls clustered in the common room, talking, shrieking, laughing, playing records. Flip stood by the balcony window thinking that she had been at the school only a few weeks and yet it seemed as though she had been there forever. She felt in her pocket for her father's latest letter that she had already read several times in the peace of the chapel. When she read his letters, those wonderful, wonderful letters, full of little anecdotes and sketches, she would look at the drawings of forlorn waifs, ragged and starving, and feel ashamed of her own misery which for the moment at any rate seemed completely unjustified. She had had a letter that morning from Mrs. Jackman, too, written on heavy, expensive paper saying that she hoped that Flip had settled down and was happy, and signed, Affectionately, Eunice. Eunice signed all her letters to Flip that way, but Flip felt no affection in them. Eunice had written that she would send Flip a weekly note, since most of the girls would be getting letters from their mothers. "Your father," Eunice had written, "will have little time for letters, and I don't want you to have the humiliation of an empty mail box." Flip read Eunice's letter, which certainly did not make her feel any better, tore it up, and threw it in the wastepaper basket.

"I love you—u—u—" the phonograph wailed.

"And then he said to me, 'Your legs are fascinating,'" Esmée was saying.

"He was the most divine boy," she heard Sally saying, "until I heard he had a whole set of false teeth and a toupee."

"During the holidays," Gloria screeched, "I smoke at least a pack of cigarettes a day."

Flip turned away from the window, slipped out of the common room, tiptoed through the big lounge, and slipped out the side door when the teacher on duty was busy talking to someone. The air was crisp and a light wind was blowing. She took deep breaths of it and walked swiftly, exulting in the unaccustomed freedom.

She climbed the hill behind the school, knowing that as she got into the pine trees clustered thickly up the mountainside she would be safe from detection. She ran until she was panting and her weak knee ached, but soon the trees got thicker and thicker and she dropped down onto the fragrant rusty carpet of fallen pine needles. As soon as she had regained her breath she walked on a little farther, rubbing her fingers lovingly over the rough, resiny trunks of the pines. She felt free and happy for the first time since she had been at school. The air was full of piney perfume; the needles were soft and gently slippery under her feet; high above her head she could see the blue sky shining in chinks and patches through the trees; and the sun sifted down to her in long golden shafts like the light in a church. She lay down on her back on the pine needles and looked up and up and it seemed that the trees pierced the sky. Oh, trees, oh, sky, oh, sun, something in her sang. Oh, beautiful, beautiful, beautiful. And she was happy.

After a while she stood up and brushed and shook the pine needles off her uniform and climbed still farther. There was a small clearing where the railroad track cut through on its zigzag way up the mountain. She crossed the track and climbed higher. She did not know where the school bounds ended and forbidden territory began; she had forgotten that there was such a thing as a boundary line, and she kept on pushing up, up the mountain.

Then, suddenly, out of nowhere, rushing in her direction with the most hideous baying she had ever heard, bounded a wild beast. Her heart leaped in terror, beating frantically against her chest, then seemed to stop entirely before she realized that the beast was Ariel.

"Ariel!" she cried, "Oh, Ariel!" as the bulldog knocked her down in the ecstasy of his greeting. "Ariel, please!" The dog began bounding around her, barking wildly, and she lay quietly on the fallen pine needles until he stopped and stood at her feet, sniffing her anxiously.

"Where's Paul?" she asked, and she was amazingly pleased to see the dog's hideous face with the drooling, undershot jaw.

Ariel barked.

Flip sat up. Then, as Ariel waited quietly, she stood up and looked around, but she could see no sign of the boy she had met down by the lake on the morning of the day she came to school.

"Paul!" she called, but there was no answer except from Ariel, who barked again, caught hold of her skirt, released it, bounded up the mountain, then came back and took her skirt in his teeth again.

"But I can't go with you, Ariel," she said. "I have to go back to school."

Ariel barked and tried again to lure her up the mountain.

"I have to go, Ariel," she told him. "I'm sure I'm out of bounds or something, being here. I have to go back to school." Then she laughed at the serious way in which she had been trying to explain the situation to the bulldog, turned away from him, and started back down the mountain. But Ariel pranced along beside her, always trying to head her back up the mountain, catching hold of her skirt or the hem of her coat, tugging and pulling, gently, but persistently.

"Ariel, you can't come back to school with me, you just can't!" Flip tried to push the dog away, but he barked, reached up, and caught hold of the cuff of her sleeve.

"Oh, Ariel!" she cried, half exasperated, half pleased because she knew the dog was going to win. "All right!"

And she turned around and headed back up the mountain.

Ariel bounded ahead of her, running on a few yards, then doubling back to make sure she was following. Soon she saw gray slate rooftops through the trees, and as Ariel led her closer she saw that the rooftops belonged to a château. When the trees cleared and Ariel began to crash through the heavy undergrowth, Flip realized that the château was old and deserted, for the shutters hung crazily by their hinges, some of the windows were boarded up, and at others the boards had come off and the glass was broken and jagged. Grass and weeds grew wild and high and late autumn flowers bloomed in undisciplined profusion. Birds flew in and out of the broken windows and as she pushed through the weeds they began calling to each other, screaming, Someone is coming! Someone is coming!

Her heart beating with excitement, Flip pressed forward, following Ariel, who suddenly leaped ahead of her, bounded across the remaining distance to the château, and disappeared. Flip pushed after him, calling, "Ariel! Ariel! Wait!" but there was no sound, no sign of life about the château except for the birds and the banging of a shutter against the gray stones. She crossed what had once been a flagstone terrace to a row of shuttered French windows. One of the shutters was open and hung by one hinge, and all the glass in the window was gone. It was through this opening that Ariel had disappeared.

Flip peered in but could see nothing through the obscurity inside.

"Ariel!" she called, then "Paul! Paul!" There was no answer and her words came faintly echoing back to her. "Ariel! Paul! Paul!"

At last she turned and started back to school.

TWO
The Page and the Unicorn

She studied French verbs in study hall that night, but because of her afternoon's adventure school seemed different and she seemed different, and even while she was dutifully memorizing a difficult subjunctive she was thinking about the château and about Ariel and Paul. And when she thought about them her heart would lift suddenly and begin to beat rapidly inside her chest so that it seemed like one of the wild, excited birds flying in and out of the broken windows of the château. She sat at her desk and said, "Please, God, let me see Paul again. Please. Please, let me see Paul again."

That night she and Gloria were already in bed, and she was lying there thinking that the next time she could escape from the school she would go back and look for Ariel and Paul again, when Erna and Jackie came in from the lavatory in their pajamas and bathrobes. Gloria was staring critically at Flip's cotton underthings folded over her chair at the foot of her bed.

"I can't stand anything but silk next to my skin," Gloria said. "Mummy's always dressed me in silk. She says she's going to send me some new silk undies from Paris."

"You and Wagner," Flip said. Jackie laughed.

Erna was tapping her foot on the floor impatiently. "Hey, we just remembered," she broke in. "You're new girls and we haven't initiated you yet."

"Oh, Erna," Gloria groaned. "Do we have to be initiated?"

Erna pulled off her barrette, pulled her hair back more tightly, and clasped the barrette again, as she always did when she felt important. "Well, you don't *have* to be, but it just means we can't accept you if you aren't. You want to be accepted, don't you?"

"Oh, okay," Gloria said. "I suppose we'll survive. Go ahead."

"Do *you* want to be accepted, Pill?" Erna asked.

Flip answered in a low voice. "Yes."

"Okay. I'll continue. Oh, first you'd better get out of bed and sit on your chairs, please."

Obediently Flip and Gloria sat on the chairs at the foot of their beds. Erna nodded in satisfaction. She stood, hands on hips, looking at them, while Jackie lounged more comfortably on her bed.

"Do you promise to keep our dormitory secrets till the death?" Erna asked.

Flip and Gloria nodded.

"And to do anything we tell you to do during the period of probation?"

Flip and Gloria nodded again.

"Good. Now we want to ask you a couple of questions."

Jackie took over. She sat up, her feet half in and half out of her woolly crimson slippers, dangling over the foot of the bed, and pointed at Gloria. "Who do you like most in the school?"

"You and Erna," Gloria answered promptly.

"I told you she'd say that." Erna nodded at Jackie.

Jackie pointed at Flip. "And you?"

"Madame Perceval."

"Percy? Well, she'll do all right." Jackie kicked one slipper onto the floor and pointed at Gloria. "Where were you born?"

"London."

"Where?"

"London."

"Where?" Erna asked.

"London."

And Jackie asked again, "Where?"

"Oh, Brazil where the nuts come from," Gloria cried in exasperation.

"Where did you say you were born?" Erna asked.

"I've told you three times," Gloria muttered.

"You seem sort of confused." Jackie kicked off the other slipper.

Erna tightened her bathrobe belt. Miss Tulip had taken her over to Lausanne that morning and the gold braces on her teeth had been tightened; her teeth hurt and her voice sounded cross. "If you don't know where you were born we certainly can't accept you. Where were you born?"

"London," Gloria mumbled sulkily.

"Are you sure?"

"Yes."

"It wasn't Brazil?"

"No."

"Why did you say it was Brazil?"

"I don't know."

"You mean you say things and you don't know why you say them?"

"No."

"But that's what you just said."

Gloria wailed, "You're trying to confuse me."

Erna put her hands in the pockets of her bathrobe and smiled tolerantly. "Why should we try to confuse you? We're just trying to find out whether or not you're sure where you were born."

"Of course I'm sure."

"Where was it?"

"London."

"All right. We'll let it go this once. But we can't have people in our room saying things without knowing why they say them. So be careful." She turned to Flip. "Okay, Pill. Where were you born?"

"Goshen, Connecticut." Warned by Gloria, Flip answered firmly while Erna and Jackie asked her seven or eight times.

Jackie slipped over the foot of the bed and pushed her feet back into her slippers. She smiled ravishingly at Flip and Gloria. "Well," she told them, "I think you've passed the preliminary examination."

Gloria stood up and stretched. "What's next?"

"You each have to prove yourself."

"How?"

"By some courageous deed. If it's good enough, then you can help with the initiation Saturday afternoon."

"The initiation?" Gloria asked suspiciously.

Erna grinned in anticipation and the light flashed on the gold braces on her teeth. "Oh, the big general initiation. All the old girls in our class are going to initiate the new girls who haven't done a magnificent enough deed by Saturday lunch. It was my idea."

Saturday afternoon, Flip thought. That was when I was planning to go look for Paul and Ariel. Well, maybe I can go tomorrow after quiet hour, though it doesn't give me too much time. I do want to see Paul again. He was nice to me by the lake and I don't think he disliked me. Going off to see Paul would be quite a deed, only I can't tell anyone.

Gloria was smiling a secret, pleased smile to herself.

"What's the joke?" Jackie asked, always eager for something to laugh at.

Gloria twined her arms about her ginger-colored head and tried to look mysterious. "I was thinking of a deed."

The door opened and Miss Tulip burst in. "Girls! The light bell rang five minutes ago. Just because I wasn't able to get here sooner is no reason for you to be out of bed. Get in at once. Do you all want deportment marks?"

"We didn't hear the bell, Miss Tulip," they chorused, making a mad scramble for their beds.

The matron waited until they were lying down and the covers drawn up, then she switched off the light. "Now I don't want to hear another sound from this room or I'll have to report you to Mademoiselle Dragonet. Good night." And the door clicked shut behind her.

Every morning before classes, all the students gathered in the Assembly Hall and one of the teachers called the roll. On Saturday and Sunday mornings call over was held as usual, although it was not followed by lessons. On Saturdays the girls trooped into the common room for sewing, and on Sundays they remained in formation and marched from the Assembly Hall down to chapel.

The morning after Erna's and Jackie's inquisition, Gloria did her courageous deed during call over. Fräulein Hauser, the gym teacher, was calling the roll. She was considered one of the strictest of all the teachers (though not so strict nor so quickly obeyed as Madame Perceval) and when it was her turn to take call over the girls stayed very quietly in their lines, answering smartly as their names were called. It wasn't long, then, this Sunday morning before Flip and most of the girls in her class, and the classes standing near, noticed that Gloria, with an expression of unconcerned innocence, was chewing something. Chewing gum was strictly forbidden, and although the girls frequently smuggled it in, none of them would have dared chew openly in the presence of a teacher.

"Anne Badeneaux," Fräulein Hauser was saying, "Moire Beresford, Anastasia Bechman, Hanni Bechman, Lischen Bechman, Jacqueline Bernstein, Esmée Bodet, Ingeborg Brandes, Dorothy Brown, Gloria Browne . . ." As Gloria answered to her name Fräulein Hauser looked at her sharply. "Gloria Browne," she said.

Gloria, still chewing, answered meekly. "Yes, Fräulein Hauser?"

"You know chewing gum is forbidden?"

"Oh, yes, Fräulein Hauser."

Fräulein Hauser held out her hand. "Come here."

Gloria detached herself from the lines of girls and went up to the platform. "Yes, Fräulein Hauser?"

Fräulein Hauser kept her hand outstretched. "Spit," she said.

Gloria spat, and there in Fräulein Hauser's upturned palm lay a gold plate attached to which were Gloria's four front teeth. Gloria turned around and smiled a brilliant, toothless smile at the assembly.

Fräulein Hauser said icily, "Get back into line. You may report to me immediately after chapel."

"Yef, Fäulein Haufer. May I haf my teef, pleef, Fäulein Haufer?" Gloria lisped. Fräulein Hauser handed her the teeth and Gloria resumed her place in line.

Throughout the entire school shoulders were shaking in ill-suppressed laughter. Erna let out one snort and turned almost purple in her effort to keep the rest of her rapture inside. Tears of mirth were streaming down Jackie's face, and even Flip felt an ache of laughter in her chest. Fräulein Hauser looked at the assembly coldly. She clapped her hands and the sound cut sharply across their laughter. "Silence!" she hissed, and her face was pale with anger. "Silence!" She stared wrathfully at the girls until their amusement was somewhat controlled. Then she went on with the roll. "Cornelli Bruch, Elizabeth Campbell, Margaret Campbell, Bianca Colantuono, Goia Colantuono, Maria Colantuono, Jeanne-Marie Crougier . . ."

After call over they marched down to the chapel where the English chaplain from Territet gave them a sermon, and after chapel Gloria was haled off by Fräulein Hauser and they did not see her until they met in the dining room for Sunday dinner. Gloria stood, looking bloody but unbowed, behind her chair as they waited for Mlle. Dragonet to say grace.

Grace ended, Mlle. Dragonet pulled out her chair, and then all the other chairs in the big dining room scraped across the floor with a sound of ocean waves. Tables were changed weekly but the girls were seated according to classes and the whole of dormitory 33 this week was together, with Solvei Krogstad and Sally Buckman. Miss Armstrong, the science teacher, was at their table for that week, but she had gone down to Montreux to have lunch with a friend who was passing through.

"Thank goodness Balmy Almy's not here!" Erna cried joyfully. "What did old Hauser do to you, Gloria?"

And Jackie was squeaking simultaneously, "How did you do it, Gloria? How did you do it? Tell us quick!"

Gloria clicked her tongue around inside her mouth and suddenly she was grinning with the four front teeth outside her lips. It was a macabre and horrible grimace. Another click and they were back in place.

"You stinker, why didn't you tell us before?" Sally asked, pushing her fingers against her nose.

"I was saving it," Gloria said. "It's my deed, so I can help with the initiation. Will it do?"

"Okay with me." Sally nodded violently.

"What happened to your teeth anyhow?" Erna asked.

"I lost 'em in the blitz. We got bombed out the night before Mummy was going to take me to the country." Gloria rubbed the tip of her tongue over her teeth. "I don't know how I ever used to put up with my own teeth. These are ever so much more useful."

"Daddy sent me back to America before the blitz,"

Sally said enviously. "I was in Detroit the whole time."

"Alphabet soup!" Gloria cried as plates were put in front of them. "The last letter left in the soup is the initial of the man you're going to marry. Mine is always X. Imagine marrying a man whose name begins with an X! At the last school I was at there was a girl who lost an eye in the blitz, and she had a glass eye she used to take out whenever she got in a row. She'd hold it in her hand and the mistress could never go on rowing her properly. But I think she used to carry it too far. One day at dinner the mistress at the table was rowing her about something and she took her eye out and put it in her glass of water. Now I call that too much. She was heaps of fun though. She got kicked out the same time I did."

"You got expelled!" Jackie exclaimed. "Ooh, what did you do, Glo?"

"Well, Pam—this girl—and I sneaked out of school one Saturday afternoon and went into town to meet Pam's brothers and of course one of the mistresses saw us and we got bounced. We didn't care though. It was a beastly school, not half as nice as this one."

"But weren't your parents upset?" Jackie asked.

"Who, Mummy and Daddy? They didn't care. There were only a couple of weeks till the summer hols and they'd have had me on their hands soon enough anyhow and this gave them a good excuse to send me off to stay with some people in Wales for the whole summer. I say, let's play Truth or Consequences, seeing Balmy Almy isn't here."

Erna, Jackie, and Sally agreed vociferously. Flip looked across at Solvei and watched her quietly eating her potatoes. She liked the Norwegian girl, who was the class president and who seemed able to assume responsibility without putting on any airs. Now Solvei said, "Let's wait till after lunch. Black and Midnight's been cocking an ear over here and looking disapproving, and you know how she hates games at the table."

Gloria stuck out her lower lip. "That old minge. Always poking her nose in other people's business. Why can't she leave us alone?"

"She has a special 'down' on our class," Sally said. "And she says the middle school's more trouble than the lower and upper schools together. What a dreep. Oh, my golly, will you look! Suet pudding again. You can feel every bite of that stuff hit the soles of your feet five seconds after you've swallowed it. I'd like a good American banana split."

"Here it is dessert"—Gloria wagged a finger at Flip— "and Pill hasn't said a single word since we sat down. What's the matter, Pill? Cat got your tongue?"

"No," Flip answered, blushing.

"I don't think I've ever heard Pill say anything." Sally grinned at Flip, but somehow there seemed to be nothing pleasant about the grin. "Can you talk, Pill?"

"Yes," Flip said.

"Well, say something then."

"There isn't—I don't—I haven't anything to say," Flip stumbled.

"Don't we inspire conversation?" Sally asked. "A lot you must think of us. Does she ever talk in the room?"

Erna was gobbling her suet pudding. "She sometimes answers if you ask her a question, if you insist. Yes, or no. That's all."

"What do you do when you go out on a date, Pill?" Sally asked. "Or don't you ever go on dates? What kind of a line do you think Pill uses on a boy?"

Flip said nothing.

"Well, what kind of a line *do* you use, Pill?" Sally persisted. "Maybe you could teach us something. Well, for John's sake, say something, can't you!"

"Oh, do leave her alone," Solvei said impatiently. "If she hasn't anything to say she hasn't anything to say."

"But how can someone *not* have something to say!" Gloria exclaimed incredulously. "There's *always* something to say. Any time I can't talk I'll be dead."

"Well, maybe Pill's dead," Sally suggested. "How about it, Pill. Are you dead?"

"No," Flip said.

Solvei interfered again on her behalf, but Flip felt that it was only from a sense of duty, that privately Solvei considered her just as much of a pill as the rest of the girls did. "Madame Perceval says your father's an artist, Philippa."

Flip nodded, then said, "Yes. He is."

"How'd Percy know? Did you tell her?" Erna asked.

Flip shook her head. "No."

"Oh, Percy always knows everything about everybody," Jackie said with admiration. "I don't know how she does it. And you can't ever get away with anything with Percy but you never mind how strict she is. Sometimes I think I love Percy almost as much as my mother."

"You have a crush on her," Sally said.

Jackie looked at the gray lump of suet pudding remaining on her plate and turned up her nose in disgust. "I merely have a great admiration for her."

"Oh, for John's sake, Jackie, I was just kidding. Can't

you take a joke? Let's change the subject. Tell us a
story, Glo. Have you heard any good ones lately?"

"Well, Esmée told me one yesterday," Gloria started.
Solvei broke in, "Not at the table. Save it for the
common room if you feel you have to tell it."

Flip looked at Solvei in gratitude. Mlle. Dragonet at
the head table stood up before Gloria could reply. All
the chairs in the dining room were scraped back and the
girls filed out.

On Sunday afternoons all the girls were supposed to
spend a rest period in their rooms, but after the rest period
there would be two hours when Flip could try to escape
and go back to the deserted château. She sat curled up on
her bed with the dog-eared calendar she carried around
with her in her blazer pocket and looked at the small
block of days that was marked off and then at all the days
and days that stretched out to be lived through somehow
before the Christmas holidays and her father would finally come. Sometimes she was afraid that the Christmas holidays would never be reached. She knew already
that the one certain thing in an uncertain world was that
time always passed; but as day followed day, each one
exactly like the other, she felt that nothing, not even
time, could put an end to their unbearable monotony.

Oh, please, God, please, God, make Christmas come
quickly, Flip prayed, her hand still moving softly over
her dog-eared calendar. And because time did not wheel
faster in its vast circle for her she became filled with
despair and homesickness and bitterness at her misery
and she shoved the book she had brought up with her off
her bed so that it fell on the floor with a thud. Across the

room Gloria yawned noisily over her required weekly letter to her mother; Erna and Jackie, as usual, were whispering and giggling together. "They're so childish," Esmée was always saying to Gloria, but she was careful to keep on good terms with Jackie because Jackie's father was a movie director.

Flip leaned over and picked up her book, smoothing out its pages in swift apology, and waited for the bell.

She hurried out of the room after quiet hour, got her coat from the cloak room, and started up the mountain. She knew that the others would think she had gone to chapel. She ran almost until she stood at the edge of the forest where the trees thinned out and mingled with the underbrush that surrounded the château, and there was the château as it had been the day before, cold and beautiful and deserted. She stood looking at the gray stones and at the birds, her heart thumping, but no Ariel came rushing toward her to knock her down with his greeting, and after a moment she began pushing her way to the château, jumping like a startled forest animal each time a twig snapped or the wind moved in the high grasses. Just as she had almost neared the decaying walls of the building she heard a low whine and there was Ariel standing in the shadow of a shutter that hung drunkenly. The shadow seemed to move and she saw that Paul was there, too, holding Ariel by the collar.

"Paul!" she called softly.

For a moment she thought Paul was going to go back into the château; then he stepped out of the shadow of the shutter and held out his hand in greeting.

"Oh," he said. "It's you."

She took his hand. "Who else would it be?"

"There are a great many girls in your school, aren't there? And you might be any of them."

"I'm not any of them," she said. "I'm me."

"How did you get here?" he asked, still holding back Ariel, who was trying to leap at Flip. "How did you find me?"

Flip retreated a little because it did not seem to her that he really was glad that she had come. "I didn't find you," she said. "Ariel found me. I went for a walk yesterday afternoon and he found me and made me come to the château."

"And you came back today," Paul said.

There was neither welcome nor rebuff in his voice, but Flip felt that she had been rejected and she said haughtily, "I'm sorry I'm not welcome. I'll leave at once."

"No, please!" Paul cried. "I said I was glad it was you. I was afraid it was someone I didn't know. I came here to be alone and I didn't want just anybody coming around."

Flip said swiftly, "If you wanted to be alone, I won't stay then. I know how it is to need to be alone. I need to be alone too."

Paul reached out for her hand again. "No, don't go, it's good to see you. I know I sounded inhospitable, but come and sit down." Still holding her firmly by the hand, he led her across the terrace to a marble bench half hidden by weeds. "Now," he said, sitting down beside her. "Do you like your school?"

She shook her head. "No. I hate it."

"And you really have to stay? You can't ask your father to take you away?"

"No." She looked down at Paul's hand beside her on the bench. It still held a warm tan from summer, and his fingers were very long and thin and at the same time gave an appearance of great strength. They were blunt at the tips, the nails square and clean. "I couldn't be with Father while he's traveling around," she said, "and I had to be somewhere and Eunice suggested this school. Father always seems to do what Eunice suggests about me . . ."

"Is she still lusting after your father?" Paul asked.

"Well, she manages to let me know that they talk on the phone all the time, and she flies to meet him whenever she can. She condescends to write me once a week."

"But she's not like your mother," Paul stated.

Flip shook her head vehemently.

"Tell me about your mother," Paul suggested, "or would that hurt?"

Flip shook her head again. "I like to talk about her. Father and I talk about her. Except when Eunice is around."

"What was she like? Was she beautiful?"

"Yes. Not like Eunice, the kind of beautiful that hits you in the teeth so you can't escape it. Subtle. And it was inside beauty, too. And she saw inside people, saw all the good parts of you. If I was feeling sorry for myself because the kids at school made me feel dumb, she made me know I could paint pictures, and that being able to draw well was a good thing, and so I'd stop being sorry for myself. She made me glad I was who I was, not someone else."

"But Eunice makes you feel not glad to be yourself?" Paul asked.

"Eunice expects me to be busy and popular and not notice when she," now Flip smiled, "lusts after Father."

Paul smiled, too. "My mother makes me feel glad to be me, too, and that isn't always easy." Again the dark look moved across his face, and he looked down.

Flip looked down, too, at Paul's feet in their heavy hiking boots. He was silent, and she continued to stare at his right foot until it twitched slightly, the way she had noticed someone's foot would do if you stared at it long enough in a subway or bus or even the classroom at school. Then he reached down and patted Ariel.

"Ariel is a beautiful dog," she said politely. "Where did you get him?"

"I found him in the street. He had been hit by a car and left there and his leg was broken. I set it myself and took care of him and now he is fine. He doesn't even limp, and when I showed him to Dr. Bejart—a friend of mine—he said he was a very fine dog."

"But that's wonderful!" Flip cried, gazing admiringly at Ariel. "How did you know about setting a leg?"

Paul looked pleased at her praise. "I intend to be a doctor. A surgeon. Of course I must go to college and medical school and everything first. Right now I don't go to school at all. I am trying to study by myself and my father is helping me, but of course I know I must go back to school sooner or later. I think that it will be later." A shadow swept over his face and it seemed to Flip as though the day had suddenly darkened.

She looked up, startled, and indeed the sun had dropped behind the mountain. She rose. "I have to go. I didn't realize it was so late. If I don't get back quickly they'll miss me."

Paul stood up too. "Do go then," he said. "If you're caught they wouldn't let you come back, would they? Will you come back?"

"Do you want me to?" Flip asked.

"Yes. When will you come?"

"I could come next Sunday. But are you sure you want me to? You don't want to be alone?"

"I can be alone all week," Paul said. "Come Sunday, then, Philippa."

She started away but turned back and said tentatively, "At home I'm called Flip . . ." and waited.

But Paul did not laugh as the girls at school had done. Instead he said, "Good-bye, Flip."

"Good-bye," she said, and started down the mountain.

When she got back to school they had noticed her long absence. Gloria turned from the group by the phonograph and demanded, "Where've you been, Pill?"

"Oh, out for a walk," Flip answered vaguely.

"Out for a walk, my aunt Fanny," Esmée Bodet said. "You've probably been mooning down in that chapel again. I think it's sacrilegious."

"Or maybe she was out on a date," Sally suggested. "I bet she was. That would be just like our Pill, wouldn't it, kids? Were you out on a date, Pill?"

"I have to wash my hands before dinner," Flip said, and as she started up the stairs she thought, Maybe you'd call it a date at that, Sally!

And she grinned as she turned down the corridor.

By the next Saturday all of the five other new girls in Flip's class had done deeds. Two of them had short-sheeted all the seniors' beds. One had wangled a big box of chocolates into the common room with the help of a cousin who lived in Montreux. Only Flip had done nothing.

Gloria tried to help her. "Maybe you could put salt in Balmy Almy's tea. I have it! You could fill all the sugar bowls with salt!"

Flip shook her head. "Where would I get the salt?"

"Well, let's think of something else then," Gloria said. "You don't know, Pill! That initiation's going to be something terrific! Maybe you could trip the Dragon up when she comes into assembly. You're on the end of the line."

Flip shook her head again.

"Well, whatever you do," Gloria warned, "don't do anything like short-sheeting a bed or making a booby trap for anyone in *our* class. They wouldn't like that."

"I won't," Flip assured her. "But I can't think of a deed, Gloria. I've tried and tried, but I just can't seem to think of anything." If only I could produce Paul and Ariel, she thought. That would bowl them over all right.

"I thought you were supposed to have such a good imagination," Gloria said. "I've done everything I can to help you, ducky, so there's nothing else for it. You'll just have to be initiated."

"I expect I'll have to," Flip agreed mournfully and with trepidation.

"I'll do what I can to keep it from being too awful," Gloria promised her magnanimously.

But she was, as Flip had known she would be, one of the most violent of the initiators.

The entire class met after lunch behind the playing fields. It was almost out of sight of the school there; only the highest turrets could be seen rising out of the trees. Erna, Jackie, and Gloria had Flip in tow.

"Don't be scared," Jackie whispered comfortingly. "It's only fun."

"I'm *not* scared." Flip was vehement. Even if she knew she was a coward she did not want anyone else to know.

It was a gray day with little tendrils of fog curled here and there about the trees. The tips of the mountains were obscured in clouds that looked heavy and soft and like snow clouds. Erna said it was too early for snow as far down the mountain as Jaman, though there might possibly be some in Gstaad, a town farther up, where the annual ski meet was held. Behind the playing fields was the most desolate spot around the school. It was rocky ground with little life; the grass was neither long nor short; just ragged and untidy and a dull rust brown in color. The only tree was dead, with one lone branch left sticking out so that it looked like a gibbet. Most of the girls clustered about the tree. Flip heard one of them asking, "What do we do?"

"Well, we put Pill through the mill first," Erna said. "Come on, peoples. Line up." She shoved and pushed at the girls until they got into line, their legs apart, then she gave Flip a not unfriendly shove. "Through the mill."

Flip bent down, held her breath, and started. With her long legs she practically had to crawl on her hands and knees as she pushed through the tunnel of legs, and her progress was slow and her bottom smarting from the slaps. She gritted her teeth and pressed on until she passed between Erna's legs at the head of the line. Erna gave her a resounding smack.

"Good for Philippa," Solvei said. "She didn't yell once."

"She has tears in her eyes," Gloria shouted.

"I have not," Flip denied.

"What are they if they aren't tears?" Esmée Bodet asked.

"It's the wind," Flip said.

"Are you ticklish?" Esmée asked.

"Yes."

Esmée rushed at her and started tickling her.

"Stop! Oh, please, stop!" Flip cried.

Esmée tickled even harder and Flip fell to the ground, laughing and gasping hysterically while all the girls shouted with amusement. But although Flip was laughing, it was the laughter of torture and she cried out whenever she could catch her breath, "Stop, oh, stop—" She laughed and laughed until she could scarcely breathe and tears were streaming down her face.

Finally Erna said, "For heaven's sake, stop, Esmée. You've done enough."

Esmée stood up while Flip lay prostrate on the ground, gasping and trying to get her breath back. She felt that now she knew what it must be like for a fish when the fisherman decides it isn't good enough and finally throws it back into the sea.

"Get up," Erna said.

Flip rolled over weakly.

"Come on. Stand up. You've got to prove yourself if you want to pass the initiation."

Flip staggered to her feet.

"All right," Erna said in a businesslike manner. "Now the inoculation. All the new girls have to be inoculated, not just you, Pill. Did you get the matches, Jack?"

Jackie nodded vigorously, so that her black curls bounced up and down. "Yes, but I only got six, one for each of them. No extras in case of emergencies. Mathilde was in a bad mood and told me to get out of the kitchen or she'd tell Black and Midnight. She acted awfully suspicious. She wanted to know what I wanted with the matches and I told her Balmy Almy wanted them for the Bunsen burners in the lab, but it didn't seem to satisfy her."

Sally Buckman gave one of the hoarse snorts that made her sound as much like a pug as she looked. "I bet she thought you were going off to smoke. Old stinker. If we could get cigarettes we could get matches."

"What're you going to do with the matches?" one of the new girls asked Erna.

"I told you. Inoculate you."

Jackie elaborated on it. "You might catch all kinds of dreadful things if you didn't get inoculated. Erna, have you got the antiseptic?"

"Right here." Erna pulled an old tube of toothpaste out of her blazer pocket. Jackie turned up the hem of her skirt and removed a needle which she handed solemnly to Erna.

"Hold out your arm, Gloria," Erna said. "You'd better take off your blazer first."

Gloria's freckled face had turned a little pale, but she rolled up her sleeve gamely and held out her arm. Erna smeared on a little of the toothpaste.

"Now." Erna waved the match. "I'll sterilize the needle." She struck the match on the sole of her shoe ("I know a boy who can strike a match on his teeth," Gloria said) and held the needle in the flame until the point became red. Then she let it cool, brandishing it in the air until the red point disappeared and there was only the black left from the carbon. Gloria turned her head away.

"It's not so bad, Glo," Jackie reassured her. "Erna's going to be a doctor, so she knows what she's doing."

Erna gave a quick, professional jab, squeezed, and a round drop of blood appeared on Gloria's arm. Gloria gave a little scream and tears came to her eyes.

"There!" Erna cried. "Now you're all immune. And it's beautiful blood. Look, peoples. Look, Gloria."

But Gloria hated the sight of blood. She glanced quickly at her arm and the small red bead, then turned away. "I have a dress that color," she said in a shaky voice.

"Next," Erna said briskly. "Come on, you, Bianca Colantuono."

One by one the new girls were inoculated until it came to Flip's turn. Then Gloria, completely recovered, cried, "Oh, let me do Pill."

Erna hesitated a moment then said, "Well, all right, if you want to. But be careful," and handed her the needle and the match.

Flip bared her arm. Gloria struck the match, but it flickered and went out.

"Oh, Glory, you sap!" Sally cried.

"I told you to be careful," Erna said, rubbing toothpaste on Flip's outstretched arm.

Jackie's face puckered into a frown. "There isn't another match. Now what should we do?"

Esmée Bodet shrugged and ran her fingers through the reddish hair she wore in a glamorous long bob. "Do it without sterilizing the needle, that's all."

Jackie hesitated. "Maybe it isn't safe. Maybe we'd better do Pill another time."

"I sterilized it good and thorough for the others," Erna said. "It ought to be all right."

"Oh, sure, it's all right," Sally cried. "Go on, Gloria."

Flip turned her head away as Gloria took her arm and jabbed at it gingerly with the needle, exclaiming with chagrined surprise, "It didn't go in."

"Try it again," Esmée urged.

Gloria jabbed again. "Oh, blow."

Erna took the needle from her. "Here, stupid. Let me do it."

"Wait a minute, Erna. She's had enough," Solvei said.

"No, she has to be properly inoculated," Erna insisted. She took the needle and punched. This time she didn't have to squeeze to draw blood. "I did it kind of hard, but it's very *good* blood, Pill," she said.

"The worst is over," Jackie promised. "You only have one more ordeal to go through."

"So, peoples," Erna said to the other new girls. "You're all through now. All we have to do is finish Pill up and then we'd better get back to the common room or someone'll be out to look for us."

"What do we do to Pill now?" they cried.

"We blindfold her and tie her to the tree," Jackie said.

"And gag her, too, don't forget," Gloria added.

"Come on, Pill, over by the tree." Erna gave her a boisterous shove.

Flip looked at the tree and it seemed more like a gibbet than ever, sticking up starkly out of the tall grasses. She remembered reading in a book once about the way you used to see gibbets along the desolate highways in England long ago; and as you drove along you would sometimes see a dead highwayman, black and awful, strung up on one of the gibbets, as a warning to thieves and murderers. She felt that this tree against which she was being forced to stand was like one of those old gallows, and for a shuddering moment her imagination told her it might have been used for that very purpose.

But no, she reassured herself. It's only a dead tree and there aren't any lonely highways nearby, only a big school that once used to be a hotel.

"Anything you'd like to say before we gag you?" Erna asked.

Flip shook her head and Sally cried, "Oh, Pill never has anything to say."

Erna tied one handkerchief over Flip's mouth, another over her eyes, and with a rope made of a number of brown woolen stockings knotted together secured her to the tree. Gloria and most of the English and American girls danced around the tree singing what to Flip was an appalling and fearful song:

> Did you ever think when a hearse goes by
> That one of these days you are going to die?

The French girls were singing a dreadful song about a corpse being dissected: *"Dans un amphithéâtre il y avait un macabre . . ."* while Erna and the rest of the girls were for some unexplained reason singing the school song.

When Gloria stopped singing she shouted, "I say, I'm tired of this. Let's go back to school and play Ping-Pong."

"How long should we leave Pill?" Jackie asked.

Erna considered. "Well, let's see."

"Not too long," Solvei put in on Flip's behalf. "She did awfully well during the initiation."

Behind her blindfold and gag Flip felt a glow of pride because she could hear from Solvei's voice that this time she really meant what she was saying.

"Well, fifteen minutes then," Erna said.

"Fifteen minutes! What are you talking about!" Esmée Bodet cried. "An hour at least."

"Well, half an hour, then," Jackie compromised.

"You're getting off easy, Pill," Gloria told the blind and dumb Flip. "Come on, kiddos. Let's play Ping and relax. Me first."

"Second!" "Third!" "Fourth!" came the cries. And, "We can come get Pill in half an hour!" "Race you back to school!"

She heard them tearing off.

She could not move or speak or see. All she could do was hear. Strangely enough, instead of being frightened, she felt an odd sense of peace. By divesting her of any voluntary action they had also divested her of any sense of responsibility. She was free simply to stand there against the tree and think what she chose until they came back. She felt that she had done well during the initiation, far better than she had expected Philippa Hunter to do and far better than they had expected the class pill to do. She was not, as yet, uncomfortable, and at first it seemed as though half an hour would pass quickly. There was very little noise in the air around her, just a faint murmur in the grasses, and occasionally when the wind shifted briefly she could hear a faint faraway burst of voices from the school.

But long before the half hour was over it seemed as though it should have been over. Through her blindfold she could not see the fog that was beginning to straggle in woolly-looking streamers about the playing fields and the grounds, but she could feel the damp seeping through her blazer and skirt and her body grow numb. Erna had bound her tightly and her muscles began to ache from standing, and the tautened stocking-rope dug into the flesh of her wrists and ankles, and the darkness became oppressive instead of peaceful. She strained against her bonds but could not move them. And now she began to be afraid, to be afraid that they had forgotten her, that no one would remember her, and she would be found there, eventually, when at last someone missed her, frozen to death.

But just as her despair turned almost to panic she heard footsteps. There they come! she thought. But it was not the running steps of a group of girls but a single pair of footsteps walking briskly.

Her heart began to thump and her imagination again thrust her onto an English highway filled with murderers and madmen. Through her gag she panted. At first she thought the footsteps were going to go on by, that whoever it was would pass without seeing her; but then she heard a low exclamation and felt deft fingers untying the blindfold and the gag.

"Well, Philippa," Madame Perceval said, and set to work unknotting the stockings. Flip stepped away from the tree and her stiff legs buckled under her and she sat down abruptly. Madame helped her up.

"Thank you," Flip whispered.

Madame looked at her and raised her eyebrows mockingly. "You look as though you'd been beset by highwaymen. What happened?"

"It was just an initiation," Flip said. "It was fun, you know."

"Was it fun?" Madame asked.

"Oh, yes."

"And what was supposed to happen next?"

"Oh, they were supposed to come back and get me in half an hour. But I'm sure I'd been there more than half an hour."

"What was the initiation about?" Madame asked. "Or is that a secret?"

"Oh, I don't think so," Flip said. "It was just our class initiating the new girls. I was the only one who really had to be initiated because all the other girls did a courageous deed, so they were exempt."

"Why didn't you do a courageous deed?"

"I couldn't think of any. The things I thought would be brave I didn't think they would, and I couldn't think of any of the same kind of things the others did."

"Things like what?"

"Things that were funny too."

"Like Gloria's spitting her teeth into Fräulein Hauser's hand?" Madame Perceval asked with a twinkle.

Flip nodded. "I don't think about things being funny until they *are* funny. My mother and father always told me my sense of humor was my weak point. It's awful to be born without a sense of humor. Sort of like being born colorblind."

"Sometimes you can grow a sense of humor, you know," Madame Perceval told her. "Now, I have an idea. Why don't you turn the tables on the girls and not be here when they come for you?"

"That would be wonderful," Flip said. "Only there's no place I'm allowed to go except the common room and they're all there. We aren't allowed in our bedrooms, and if I hide in the bathroom Miss Tulip will come and knock on the door."

"Come along with me to my room," Madame Perceval said. "You're allowed to be there if I invite you."

"Oh, that would be wonderful!" Flip cried. "But—but you were going somewhere."

"Just for a walk, and it's colder than I thought it was. Legs unlimbered?"

"Yes, thank you." Flip grinned and shook out her gangly legs.

"Come along then." Madame Perceval took her arm in a friendly way and they set out for the school. They walked in silence, Flip desperately trying to think of something to say to the art teacher to show that she was grateful. Every once in a while she stole a look at Madame Perceval's face, and it was serene and quiet and Flip remembered the way she had looked that evening when she leaned against the tree and looked out over the lake.

"We'll go in the back way," Madame Perceval said, "so we'll be sure not to bump into anyone." She took Flip's hand and opened the small back door and together they crept upstairs like two conspirators. Flip felt ecstatically happy.

Madame lived on the top floor of the building near the art studio. She was the only person who slept on the fifth floor except for the cook and the maids, who were in the opposite wing of the building. Most of the teachers had single rooms distributed about the school among the girls so that there was at least one teacher to each corridor. Madame Perceval had two curious rooms in one of the turrets, and a tiny kitchen as well. She led Flip into her sitting room. It was octagonal; four of the walls were filled with books; the other four were covered with prints. Flip recognized many of her favorites, two Picasso *Harlequins*, Holbein's *Erasmus*, Lautrec's *Maybe*, Seurat's *Study for the Grande Jatte*, a stage design by Inigo Jones, Van Gogh's *Le Café de Nuit*, Renoir's *Moulin de la Galette*. Flip looked at them, enthralled.

Madame Perceval smiled. "I like it too," she said. "It's a hodgepodge, but I like it. This bit of privacy is the one privilege I ask for being Mademoiselle Dragonet's niece. Sit down and I'll brew us a pot of tea." She moved the screen away from the grate, stirred up the coals, and added some more. Flip sat down on a stool covered with a patch of oriental rug and stared into the fire. Behind her she could hear Madame Perceval moving about in her tiny kitchen, and then she was aware that the art teacher was standing behind her. "A penny for your thoughts, Philippa," Madame Perceval said lightly.

Flip continued to stare into the fire. "I was thinking how happy I was, right now, this very minute," she said. "And if I could always be happy the way I am now, I wouldn't mind school so much."

"Do you mind school so very much?" Madame Perceval asked.

Flip realized that she had expressed herself far more fully than she had intended. "Oh, no," she denied quickly. "I don't think I've ever been anywhere that was so beautiful. And at night I can look down the mountain to the lake and it's like something out of a fairy tale. And when there's a fog and sometimes you can see the Dents du Midi and then they disappear and then you can see them again—that's like a fairy tale too. And the kids say we go to Lausanne and Vevey and Gstaad and places at half term and we're going to climb the Col de Jaman on Tuesday as the new girls' welcome and I expect that'll be beautiful only I'm not very good at climbing . . ." Her voice trailed off.

"Fräulein Hauser says there's something wrong with one of your legs," Madame Perceval said abruptly. "What is it?"

"I broke my knee."

"How?"

"In an automobile accident."

There was something strained and tense in Flip's voice and Madame Perceval went quietly into the kitchen and poured water from the now-hissing kettle into a small earthenware teapot. She brought the teapot into her living room and two delicate Limoges cups and saucers and placed them on the low table in front of the fire by a plate of small cakes.

"Tell me about the automobile accident, Philippa," she said.

Flip took a cup and saucer and stirred her tea very carefully. "It was a year ago. It will be a year . . ." she buried her face in her hands, ". . . tomorrow." She took her hands down from her face and dropped them in her lap. Madame Perceval sat looking quietly into the fire, her feet on the low brass hearth rail, and waited. At last Flip said, "Mother and Father and I were driving over to Philadelphia to spend the weekend with some friends, and it began to snow, a very early snow which wasn't even predicted, and it was mixed in with sleet and rain. The windshield wipers hardly worked. And some crazy driver tried to pass a truck and skidded and there was an accident. The people in the other car weren't hurt, and it was all their fault. The truck driver was killed." She paused again. "And my mother was killed."

Madame Perceval continued to look into the fire, but Flip knew that she was listening.

"Father was cut and bruised," Flip continued, "and my kneecap was broken. It's really all right now, though, except it gets sort of stiff sometimes. But I never was any good at running and things anyhow."

The gong for tea began to ring. It reverberated even back into Madame Perceval's room as the maid rode up and down in the skeleton of the elevator. Flip put her cup and saucer down on the table and her hand was trembling. "There's the gong for tea," she said.

"Do you want to go down?" Madame Perceval asked.

"No."

Madame Perceval reached for a telephone on one of the bookshelves; Flip had not noticed it before. "One of the advantages of the school's having been a hotel," Madame said, "is that all the teachers have telephones connected with the switchboard downstairs. I'll call Signorina del Rossi—I think she's in charge today—and tell her to excuse you from tea. We won't tell anyone and we'll have all the girls wondering where you are and that ought to be rather fun."

"Oh, that's wonderful!" Flip cried. "Oh, Madame, thank you."

"Hello, Signorina," Madame said on the telephone. "Madame Perceval." Then she launched into Italian, which Flip did not understand. There was a gool deal of laughter, then Madame hung up and took Flip's cup. "All right, little one. Let me give you some more tea."

So Flip sat there and drank tea and ate Madame Perceval's cakes and felt warmth from far more than the fire seep into her.

Madame passed her the cake plate. "Have another. They come from Zürcher's in Montreux and they're quite special. I allow myself to have them every once in a while. What do you want to be after you leave school, Philippa? An artist?"

Flip bit into a small and succulent cake, crisp layers of something filled with mocha cream. "I think so. But my father says it's probably just because he paints and he doesn't want me to do anything just because he does it. Anyhow, he says he's not at all sure I have enough talent."

Madame laughed and filled Flip's teacup for the third time. "I like your father's work. Especially his illustrations for children's books."

"Oh, do you know them?" Flip was excited.

Madame reached up to the bookshelves and pulled down a copy of *Oliver Twist*.

"Oh!" Flip said. "Oh, that's one of my favorites!"

Madame replaced the book. "Mine too. I keep your father's things next to Boutet de Monvel, which shows you how much I think of him."

It was one of the most beautiful afternoons Flip had spent in a long time. She did not once think a dreary or bitter thought, such as, I'm the most unpopular girl in the school. That ought to make Eunice happy. When the bell rang for dinner and Madame sent her downstairs, for once she was almost eager to get to her place in the dining room. Tables were changed on Thursday, and she was at an unchaperoned table with only Erna from her room this week, but all the girls in the class whispered excitedly as she came in, "Philippa!" "Pill!" "Here she is!" "Where have you been?" "What happened to you?"

She stood decorously behind her chair and waited for Mlle. Dragonet to say grace. Erna burst out as they sat down, "Pill, we've been frantic! We thought you'd been kidnapped or something. If you hadn't come to dinner we were going to tell Signorina you were lost. What on earth happened to you?"

Flip actually grinned. "To me? What do you mean? Nothing."

"Stop being so smug," Esmée Bodet said, tossing her hair back. "I told you she'd just sneaked off somewhere and there wasn't any point worrying about her."

"But how could she just sneak off somewhere!" Erna cried. "We tied her so she couldn't possibly get away."

"That's right," Flip agreed.

"What happened, Pill, what happened?" Erna begged.

"Oh," Flip said airily, "my fairy godmother came and rescued me."

"But where were you during tea? Jackie and I missed tea looking for you and Signorina almost gave us deportment marks because we wouldn't tell her what we were doing."

"Oh, I went over to Thônon," Flip told her, "and had tea with a duke."

Erna and the other girls were looking at her with something like respect and for the first time Flip felt that she had triumphed.

The next day was not easy for Flip, but somehow the fact that Madame Perceval knew it was the anniversary

of her mother's death helped. She thought she saw the
art teacher looking at her during chapel, calmly, firmly,
as though to give her strength.

And it was Sunday, so she could escape the school and
take her grief and go up the mountain with it, alone. And
then she could go to the château. Paul was expecting her,
and that, too, gave her strength.

"Hello, Flip!" Paul shouted as soon as he saw her.

"Hello!" she shouted back. She hurried across the rough
ground to where he was waiting for her by the loose
shutter. But when she reached him they both fell silent,
somehow overcome with shyness. Paul ran his fingers over
the flaking paint of the shutter, and Flip searched her
mind for something to say. She hoped that any trace of
the tears she had shed while she was climbing up through
the trees had been wiped away by the wind. She thought
of telling Paul that her mother had died a year ago, but
something in his eyes made her sure that it would not be
a good idea. Despite Paul's loving mention of his parents,
there was always grief in his eyes. She had no idea why,
except that Paul's eyes told her that he had endured
something terrible, and that his own pain was all he
could bear.

Gloria or Sally or Esmée would know what to say to a
boy, Flip thought. They had all been on dates; but Flip
could not think of words that would not sound self-
pitying; or, even worse, foolish.

Then she looked at Paul's face, at the shadowed eyes
and the strong sensitive line of the jaw, and the way his
mouth was tight, as though his teeth were clenched, and
she felt that the things that Gloria or Sally or Esmée
would say to Paul would not be the right things. She

knew that they would say them, anyhow, unaware of their wrongness, and that they would think that Paul was handsome and romantic; but as she watched Paul standing there silently she felt with a sudden rush of confidence that he would prefer someone whose words were clumsy and inadequate, but honest, to someone whose words were glib and superficial; and this sudden sureness broke her fear of the silence and she no longer sought frantically for words.

Then, because there was no longer any need to fear the silence, she was able to break it. "Where's Ariel?"

"He stayed home with my father," Paul said.

"Are you sure you don't mind because I came back?" she asked. "Because if you'd rather be alone I'll just go on walking somewhere."

"No—no—" Paul said quickly. "I'm sorry. We live alone and sometimes my father goes a whole day without saying anything. Of course some days he talks a great deal and reads to me, but I get used to being with someone and not talking."

"Who is your father?" Flip asked. "Where do you live?"

"My father's a professor of philosophy. He used to teach in Lausanne but now he's at the Sorbonne. At least he's there usually, I mean. This year he's on a sabbatical leave and he's writing a book. That's why he doesn't talk much. He spends hours in his study and then he comes to the table and I don't think he has any idea what he eats. He just sits there and goes on thinking."

"Where do you live?" Flip asked again.

"At the gate house to the château. But I stay over here most of the time and then I'm sure I won't disturb

my father and he won't notice me and think I ought to
be in school. Besides, there's something I want to find
out."

"What?"

Instead of answering, Paul asked, "Would you like to
see the château?"

"Oh, yes."

"You aren't afraid of bats and mice and rats and
beetles and spiders and things, are you?"

"Why?"

"There are a great many inside."

Flip *was* afraid of bats and mice and rats and beetles
and spiders and things; but she was more afraid of
Paul's scorn, so she said, "I don't mind them."

Paul looked at her as though he knew that she minded
very much indeed; then he slipped behind the shutter
into the château, laughing back at her and calling,
"Come on, Flip."

Flip followed him into a great hall with a fireplace the
size of a room. The hall was bare and colder than outside.

"There are rooms and rooms," Paul said. "I've tried
to count them, but each time I come out with a different
number. There are so many little turns and passages.
There are all these dozens of rooms and only one bathroom and it's as big as our living room in the gate house.
And the tub is the size of a swimming pool. But if you
want hot water you have to build a fire in a sort of stove
under the tub. Oh, come, Flip, I want to show you something."

Flip followed Paul down a labyrinth of passages into
a small round room that must have been in one of the
turrets. It had stained glass windows and, unlike most of

the rooms, was not completely empty. In the center of the room was an old praying-chair with a monogram worked into the mahogany. Something was moving in the red velvet of the cushion and she leaned over and there was a tiny family of mice, the babies incredibly pink and soft.

"Oh, Paul!"

"We mustn't disturb them, but I thought you'd like to see them. I found them only yesterday," Paul said. "In the spring I'll show you birds' nests. Last spring in Paris I found a sparrow with its wing broken and I took care of it and helped it to learn to fly again and after that it came to my window every morning for crumbs. I kept them in the drawer of my desk and it used to fly through the window and over to the desk and jump up and down and squawk until I opened the drawer. I had a cat, too, who'd lost his tail in a fight. The concierge in our house is keeping the cat for me till I come back."

Flip bent over the mice again. "They're so terribly sweet. I don't see why people are afraid of mice."

"They don't know them," Paul said. "People are always afraid of things they don't know. This room used to be the private chapel of the lady of the château, Flip, and that prie-dieu is where she used to kneel to pray."

"How do you know, Paul?" Flip asked.

"My father told me. For a man who spends hours just sitting and thinking about philosophy he knows a tremendous amount about anything you can think of to ask him."

Flip crossed to one of the windows and looked out through a pane of blue glass onto a blue world. The sun was beginning to slip behind the mountain and she said, "I have to go now, Paul."

"Will you come next week?" Paul asked.

"Yes, I could come on Saturday next week. I could come earlier in the afternoon if you'd like."

"I'd like it very much," Paul said. "Do you really have to go now?"

"I think I'd better."

"There are so many things I want to ask you. Do you like to ski?"

"I don't know how yet. But I'm going to learn this winter. Do you like it?"

"More than anything in the world. I never can wait for the snow and they say it will be late this year. Do you like to read?"

"I love it."

"I do too. Do you like the theater?"

"Oh, yes."

"So do I. We seem to like a lot of the same things. Maybe that's why I can talk to you. Usually with other people I feel strange and as though there were a wall between us, or as though we were speaking a different language, even when we're really not. I can speak four languages, yet I can't talk at all to most people. But you're different. I can talk to you so easily, and this is only the third time we've seen each other."

"I know," Flip said, looking at the mice again instead of at Paul, at the tiny pink babies and at the little gray mother with her bright, frightened eyes. "I can talk to you, too, and I can't talk to anybody at school."

Paul turned away from the mice. "We're disturbing her. She's afraid we might take her babies. Come on. We'd better go downstairs. I don't want you to get into trouble at your school. They'd be very unpleasant if they knew you'd been here."

"You seem to know a lot about girls' schools," Flip said.

Paul started to lead the way back through the maze of corridors. "Institutions in general are similar," he said loftily. Then, "You really will come on Saturday, Flip?"

"Come hell or high water," Flip promised, feeling very bold.

Paul held out his hand to say good-bye and Flip took it. She felt that Paul did not realize that he was shaking hands with the most unpopular girl in the school.

She walked back to school, thoughtfully.

She had been happy while she was with Paul, and while, underneath the happiness, there was still an ache of grief, there was also an acceptance. Her mother was dead. She would always miss her; she would always feel the loss of her mother's confidence in her value; but she knew now that the confidence must come from within herself. Even if her mother had not died, Flip would have had to stop clutching at her mother's faith in her, and find her own.

At the clearing at the edge of the woods she stopped to make sure no one was around, and then ran across the open space, trying not to get out of breath because she knew that if she went into the common room, still panting, her cheeks flushed, someone would notice and try to find out where she had been. She wanted nothing more than to tell someone about Paul; she had always wanted to share her happiness with the world, but she knew that if she was to see him again she had to keep him a secret.

And he wants to see me again! she thought exultantly.

He's not frightening the way I always thought being alone with a boy would be. It was just like talking to anyone, only nicer, and he wants to see me again!

She had seen a tapestry once, in the Metropolitan Museum in New York, of a young page standing with a unicorn. The page was tall and slender with huge dark eyes and thick dark hair, and Paul reminded her of him. He had the same unselfconscious grace, and when his hand rested on Ariel's collar it was with the same self-assured nobility that the hand of the page rested on the unicorn's neck. She was pleased and excited that she had thought of the resemblance. And I can imagine that Ariel's magic like the unicorn, she thought. After all, it was he who brought me to Paul.

Tuesday was fine, so Flip's class was taken by Fräulein Hauser and Madame Perceval on the promised trip to the Col de Jaman. From the playing fields at school they could see the Dent de Jaman rising high and white above the Col, and Erna said that in the spring they would climb the Dent itself. It looked very high and distant to Flip and she was just as happy that they were to start with the Col, which was the flat high ridge from which the Dent pierced upward into the sky. It was to be an all-day trip. They were to be excused from all classes and would start right after call over.

"It's almost worth having new girls," Erna shouted to Jackie, "to get an excursion like this!"

They lined up on the cement walk under the plane trees while Fräulein Hauser called the roll. They did not have to choose partners, and this was a relief to Flip, because even the most polite girls in the class seemed to her to look annoyed when they were stuck with her, and on Thursday when one of the girls had been in the infirmary with a cold and there had been an odd number in the class, Flip had been left without a partner altogether, and Miss Armstrong, who was taking the walk, had had to say, "Philippa, go walk with Solvei Krogstad and Margaret Campbell."

Fräulein Hauser blew her whistle and they started off. At first they walked along the road that wound up the mountain past the school, passing chalets and farms and an occasional villa. Madame Perceval led the way, with two of the new girls. Fräulein Hauser brought up the rear with Erna and Jackie. Flip straggled along with Gloria and Sally and Esmée Bodet, not particularly wanting to walk with them, wanting even less to walk alone. After a while Madame Perceval turned off the road and they plunged into the shade of the forest and now Flip was able to pull aside and walk by herself without feeling conspicuous. Her feet were almost noiseless as she walked over a deep layer of fallen pine needles and moist leaves and she noticed that even Gloria and her group were walking more quietly. Gloria saw Flip and beckoned to her, but Flip no longer felt any need to straggle along beside anyone, and continued quite happily to walk by herself, Philippa alone with the forest.

Here the trees were taller and of greater girth than the trees in the woods behind the school, and the sun came through them in delicate arrows, piercing the dark iris of Jackie's left eye, bringing out the ruddy lights in Madame Perceval's hair, striking the gold of the braces on Erna's teeth. Then at last they emerged beyond the forest and came out into pastureland. Now, as they climbed, the trees would be below them; when they were high enough the trees would seem like a girdle about the mountains. The rough grass was broken here and there by rocks and the girls would climb onto them and leap off, laughing and shouting. Sometimes they passed cows or goats; constantly Flip could hear the faint ringing of the animals' bells.

Fräulein Hauser blew her whistle. "We will stop here for lunch," she announced.

They sprawled about on the largest rocks, opening their lunches. They had bread and cheese, an apple and an orange, some sweet biscuits, and a little twist of paper containing salt and pepper for the hard-boiled egg in the bottom of the bag. Madame Perceval carried a canteen of coffee and a flask of brandy in case of emergency, and they each had a canteen filled with fresh water from the school.

Flip sprawled on a small rock near Madame Perceval, who was laughing and joking with a group of girls. She smiled warmly at Flip and tried to draw her into the conversation, but Flip sat there shyly, afraid that if she spoke she would say the wrong thing and someone would laugh at her. One of the girls was missing salt and pepper from her package, and Flip offered hers. At the careless "Thanks, Pill," Madame Perceval looked at Flip intently, not missing the quick flush that always came to her face at the use of the nickname.

After they had finished eating they started to climb again. Now the way became rockier and steeper, and Flip and several of the less athletic girls were panting and ready to flop down on the turf long before they reached the flat plateau of the Col. Flip's throat was dry and aching and her heart thumped painfully against her ribs.

But when they finally reached the summit, she realized that the climb was more than worth it. She dropped onto a patch of rust-colored grass; the sky was incredibly blue above her and the Dent de Jaman rose out of the Col like a white castle, like the home of the snow queen in Andersen's fairy tale. A small wind blew across her hot cheeks and the ache in her knee dwindled and the sunlight made the old, rusty grass seem almost golden. She closed her eyes and the sunlight flickered over her eyelids and the grass pricked through her uniform into her skin and she rolled over and laid her cheek against a flat gray rock and somewhere, far off, she heard a bird singing.

Although it was not anywhere near tea time according to the school clock, they had eaten lunch shortly after eleven and Madame Perceval and Fräulein Hauser started handing around packets of marmalade sandwiches. At the sound of the whistle Flip rose and straggled over to the girls surrounding the teachers. She stood on the outskirts, still looking about her at the sky and the mountains and the snow, and feeling that wonderful surge of happiness at the beauty that always banished any loneliness or misery she might be feeling. Somehow a miscount had been made in the school kitchen when the tea was packed and Solvei and Jackie, and of course Flip, the last one on the outskirts, found themselves without anything to eat for tea. A small chalet stood across the ridge and Madame Perceval said, "I know Monsieur and Madame Rasmée. They're used to serving meals to amateur mountain climbers and I know they could take care of these girls. Suppose I take them over."

"It seems the only thing to do," Fräulein Hauser agreed.

So Flip found herself walking across the rough ground with Madame Perceval, Solvei, and Jackie, her pleasure in this unusual adventure marred by her awareness of the longing glances Jackie cast at Erna, and Solvei at her best friend, Maggie Campbell.

Madame Perceval said a few words to the pleasant woman who met them at the chalet and in a few minutes the girls found themselves sitting at a small table in front of an open fire. They stripped off their blazers.

"All right, girls," Madame Perceval said. "Have a good tea and come back as soon as you've finished."

"Oh, yes, Madame." They smiled at her radiantly as she left them. Only Madame Perceval would have allowed them to enjoy this special treat unchaperoned.

"I wish Percy taught skiing instead of Hauser," sighed Jackie. "She's much better."

Solvei nodded. "Once, last winter when Hauser had the flu, Percy took skiing and it was wonderful."

"She's always one of the judges at the ski meet," Jackie continued, "and then there's Hauser, and the skiing teacher from one of the other schools, and two professional skiers. It's wonderful fun, Pill. There aren't any classes, like today, and we all go up to Gstaad for the meet and have lunch up there and there are medals and a cup and it's all simply *magnifique*."

Flip thought of the skis Eunice had given her and somehow she felt that she might be good at skiing. And she was happy, too, because suddenly Jackie and Solvei seemed to be talking to her, not at her and around her, and she opened her mouth to tell them about the skis Eunice had given her, skis that had belonged to Eunice but which she had discarded; Eunice did not really care for skiing. *Because she doesn't look her best in ski clothes,* Flip thought unkindly. "My skis—" she started to say to Solvei and Jackie, when suddenly she closed her mouth and she felt the blood drain from her face and then flood it, because there, coming in at the door, was a tall stooped man, and with him, slender and dark, was Paul.

THREE
The Escape from the Dungeon

Paul saw her almost at once and quickly shook his head, and Flip heaved a sigh of relief. Thank goodness, oh, thank goodness, Jackie and Solvei had their backs to the door and had seen neither Paul nor his signal.

But Jackie said, "What's the matter, Pill? You look as though you'd seen a ghost."

Flip pretended to choke and said, "I just swallowed the wrong way. May I have the butter, please, Solvei?"

On Thursday Flip received one of the proprietary letters from Eunice that always upset her. Luckily she was assigned to Madame Perceval's table that day, and this special stroke of luck cheered her a little, for Madame Perceval's tact and humor seemed to act like a magnet drawing everyone into a warm circle of friendliness and sympathy. Erna was with her again and said as they sat down after grace, "We seem to stick together like glue, don't we, Pill?"

Flip nodded and grinned, because Erna's tone had been friendly.

During dinner they began discussing their parents. Esmée Bodet's father was a lawyer. Erna's father was a surgeon and had done operations on the battlefields. Polly Huber, an American girl from Alabama who had been at the school for three years, had a father who was a newspaperman, and Maggie Campbell's father taught Greek at the University of Edinburgh.

"And your father's a painter, isn't he, Pill?" Erna asked.

"Yes."

"Well, our house needs painting. Do you think he'd do it cheap for us since I know you?"

All the girls laughed loudly except Flip, who colored angrily and looked down at her plate with a sulky expression.

After dinner, when everybody stood up, Madame Perceval said quietly to Flip, "Please wait, Philippa." And all the girls exchanged glances, because that was the tone Madame used when she was not pleased and intended to say so. Flip stood nervously behind her chair and looked down at the table with the empty dessert dishes and the crumbs scattered about and at Madame Perceval's coffee cup with a small amount of dark liquid left in the bottom.

"Philippa," Madame said gravely when they had the dining room to themselves except for the maids who were clearing away, "I haven't seen you a great deal with the other girls, but several of the teachers have told me that you are always off somewhere sulking and that your attitude is unfriendly in the extreme."

"I don't mean to sulk," Flip said. "I didn't know I sulked. And I don't mean to be unfriendly. I don't, truly, Madame." If I had been thinking of Paul instead of Eunice I wouldn't have behaved the way I did, she thought.

"When Erna suggested that your father paint her house she was making a joke and you took it seriously and looked hurt and wounded."

"I know," Flip said. "It was stupid of me."

"But you always do it, don't you?"

"Yes," Flip admitted. "I guess I do, most of the time."

"I know you're not happy here, Philippa, but when you make it so easy for the girls to tease you, you can't blame them for taking advantage of it. Girls can be very cruel, especially when they get the idea that someone is 'different.' "

"But I *am* different," Flip said desperately.

"Why?"

"I'm so clumsy and I'm the tallest girl in the class. I'm as tall as lots of the seniors. And I fall over things and I'm not good at athletics, and I wasn't blitzed or underground or anything during the war."

Now Madame Perceval sounded really severe. "I didn't expect to hear you talk quite so foolishly, Philippa. You are tall, yes, but you can turn that into an advantage later on. And perhaps right now you're a little awkward, but you'll outgrow that. Incidentally, have you forgotten that Maggie Campbell's sister, Liz, has a brace on her leg? And she's one of the most popular girls in her class. And as for being blitzed or underground, remember that the girls who are in the difficult and defensive position are the German girls. They've had a hard time of it here, some of them. It wasn't easy for Erna, for instance."

"Yes," Flip persisted stubbornly, "but they were all in it and I wasn't in it at all."

"Neither were the other Americans," Madame said sharply. "I'm beginning to realize what the other teachers meant."

Flip looked as though Madame Perceval had struck her. She pleaded, "Please don't hate me because I've been the—the way I've been. Please. I'll try not to be. I'll try to be different. I do try. I just don't seem to know how. But I'll try harder. And I know it's all my own fault. Truly."

"Very well," Madame Perceval said. "Go on back to the common room now until time for study hall."

"Yes, Madame." Flip started to leave, but when she got to the dining room she turned and said desperately, "Madame, thank you for telling me. I—I guess I needed to be told how awful I am."

For the first time, Madame Perceval smiled at her, but all she said was, "All right, Philippa. Run along." And she gave her a little spank.

Flip spent the rest of the week waiting for Saturday and sighed with relief when Paul was at his usual place by the shutter when she reached the château. Ariel ran dashing to meet her, jumping up and down and barking. I feel as though I'd come home, Flip thought as she waved at Paul.

"Hello, Flip!" Paul called. "Down, Ariel! Down! Come here this instant, sir!"

Ariel went bounding back to Paul, who held him by the collar and Flip thought again how much he looked like the page in the tapestry.

"Hello," she said, her heart leaping with pleasure because Paul was so obviously glad to see her. She had dug Eunice's gift of Chanel No. 5 out of her bottom drawer and put a little behind her ears and had brushed her hair until it shone.

"Come on," Paul urged. "I want to show you something." He went into the château and Flip and Ariel followed. They went across the empty hall and up the wide stairs, then down a broad corridor and up more stairs, and it seemed that every time Paul led her down a dim passage there was another flight of stairs at the end. At last he opened a door and started up a very steep, circular iron stairway. Openings were cut in the thick stones of the walls and through them Flip could see the sky, very blue, and puffs of snowy clouds. The stairs were white with bird droppings and Flip could hear the birds just above their heads. A swallow sat on the stones of one of the openings and watched them. Ariel laboriously climbed up three steps, then sat down to wait, a patient expression on his ferocious bulldog's countenance. Flip followed Paul on up. At the top of the stairs was a small platform and more openings looking out over the country on all four sides. The birds flew in and out, scolding excitedly. Flip rushed to one of the windows and there was the valley of the Rhone spread out before her, Montreux, Vevey and Lausanne, lying in a pool of violet shadows, and the lake like melted silver, and across the lake the mountains rising proudly into the sky, with the snow descending farther and farther down their strong flanks in ever-lengthening streaks.

"Like it?" Paul asked.

"Oh, yes!" Flip breathed. "Oh, Paul—"

"This is my place," Paul said. "I never thought I'd bring anyone here. But I knew you'd feel about it the way I do."

Paul leaned back against the cold stones of the turret wall, his scarlet sweater bright against the gray stone. "Still worrying about that Eunice?"

"I can't help it," Flip said.

"School any better?"

"No."

"Still hate it?"

"Yes."

"Well, I don't blame you. It must be very unpleasant living in an institution."

"I don't think it's the school," Flip told him with unwilling honesty. "I think it's just me. Lots of the girls love it."

Paul shook his head. "I don't think I'd ever like a place where I couldn't leave when I chose."

"I'd like it better," Flip said with difficulty, "if anybody liked me. But nobody does." She leaned her elbows on one of the ledges and stared out over the valley toward the Dents du Midi so that she would not have to look at Paul.

"Why don't they like you?" Paul asked.

"I don't know."

"But I like you."

Flip did not insult him by saying "Do you really?" Instead she asked, "Why do you like me, Paul?"

Paul considered. "I knew right away that I liked you, so I never bothered to think why. I just—well, I like the way you look. Your eyes are nice. I like the way you see things. And I like the way you move your hands. You could be a surgeon if you wanted to. But you want to be an artist."

"Yes," Flip said, blushing at his words. "I want to paint and paint. Everything in the world. Mostly people, though. Paul—" she asked hesitantly.

"What?"

"It doesn't make you like me any less because—"

"Because what?"

"Because the girls at school don't like me . . ."

Paul looked at her severely. "You can't think much of me if you think I'd stop liking you just because a few silly girls in school haven't any sense. If they don't like you, it's because they don't know you. That's all."

"It's funny," Flip said, "how you can know someone for years and years and never know them and how you can know someone else all at once in no time at all. I'll never know Eunice. I'll always feel funny with her. But the very first day I saw you I felt as though I knew you, and when I'm with you I can talk . . . I'd better go now. It's getting awfully late. See how dark the towns are getting down by the lake."

"Can you come back tomorrow?" Paul asked.

"Yes. I know they'll catch me sooner or later and then it'll be awful, but I'll come till they catch me."

"They wouldn't give you permission to see me if you asked?"

"Oh, no! Nobody except seniors is allowed to see boys —except brothers."

"Well, I'll think of something." Paul sounded so convincing that Flip almost believed he really would be able to work out a plan. "Come on," he said. "Ariel and I'll walk as far as the woods with you, but I think it would be dangerous if I went any farther. We mustn't run any risk of being seen together."

As she followed Paul down from the tower Flip felt so happy over their friendship that she almost wanted to cry, it was so wonderful. She said good-bye to Paul at the edge of the woods and was nearly back at school when something terrible almost happened. She had cleared the ring of trees and was scurrying across the lawn, when Martha Downs and Kaatje van Leyden came around the corner of the building. Flip saw them and started to hurry toward the side door, but Martha called her. Flip was awed by both of them at the best of times —Martha, the beautiful and popular head girl of the school, and Kaatje, the equally popular and formidable games captain and head monitor; and Flip knew that this was anything but the best of times. She felt as though her guilt were sticking all over her like molasses.

"Where are you off to in such a hurry?" Martha asked.

"Nowhere," Flip answered. "I just went for a walk."

"All by yourself?"

"Yes."

"Couldn't you find anyone to go with you?"

"I wanted to be by myself," Flip said.

"That's all right," Kaatje interposed kindly. "We all like to be by ourselves once in a while. She wasn't breaking any rules."

Flip was sure that they would ask her where she had been, but Martha said instead, "You're Philippa Hunter, aren't you?"

Flip nodded.

"I'm glad we bumped into you," Martha told her. "I've been meaning to look you up. I had a letter a few days ago from a friend of my mother's, Mrs. Jackman."

"Oh," Flip said.

"And she asked me to keep an eye on you."

"Oh," Flip said again. Why did Eunice have to pursue her even at school?

"She said she was a very dear friend of your father's, and that it was through her you had come here."

That's right, Flip thought. It's all because of Eunice.

But she knew she couldn't really blame Eunice and anyhow, now that there was Paul, being miserable while she was actually at the school didn't matter so much anymore.

"Everything all right?" Martha asked. "You're all settled and everything?"

"Yes, thank you."

"Anything I can do for you?"

"No, thank you."

"Well, if you ever want me for anything, just come along and give a bang on my study door."

"I will. Thank you very much," Flip said, knowing that she wouldn't. And she went back into the common room and sat at the big billiard table, a legacy from the days when the school had been a hotel, and tried to write a letter to her father. But she could not concentrate. Images of Eunice kept crowding themselves into her mind. Eunice. Eunice and her father. Once Eunice had even said something to her about her father being young and probably marrying again—but not Eunice! Please, not anybody, but especially please, not Eunice!

The next morning when she woke up, Flip's throat was raw and her head was hot and when she opened her mouth to speak her voice came out in a hoarse croak.

"You'd better report to the nurse," Erna told her.

Flip shook her head violently. "I'm all right. Just getting a cold."

"Sounds as though you'd got one, ducky," Gloria said.

"Oh, well, it's nothing," Flip creaked in a voice like a rusty hinge.

Nothing, she thought, nothing must keep her from going up to the château to see Paul.

Fortunately it was Sunday and breakfast was unsupervised; she might have escaped detection if it hadn't been for Madame Perceval. Madame Perceval was planning an art exhibit and, after chapel, she came into the common room and walked over to the corner where Flip sat reading *Anna Karenina*.

"Philippa," she said as Flip scrambled clumsily to her feet.

"Yes, Madame?"

"I want to use two of your paintings in my exhibit and you haven't signed either of them. Come up to the studio with me and do it now."

"Yes, Madame," Flip croaked.

"What on earth is the matter with your voice, child?"

"Oh, nothing, Madame, really. I'm just a little hoarse."

"After you've finished signing your pictures you'd better report to Mademoiselle Duvoisine."

Mlle. Duvoisine was the school nurse, and since she was a special friend of Miss Tulip's, Flip rather distrusted her. "Oh, no, Madame, I'm all right, truly. Please, I promise you."

"We'll leave that up to Mademoiselle Duvoisine. Come along, please, Philippa."

As they walked along the corridor and started up the stairs Madame Perceval said in her pleasant voice,

"You've been trying hard, Philippa. Keep it up."

Flip bowed her head and muttered something unintelligible, blushing with pleasure that her efforts had been noticed.

After she had signed her pictures, writing HUNTER carefully in one corner the way her father did, Madame Perceval walked back to the infirmary with her. Mlle. Duvoisine was sitting at the infirmary desk, knitting a heather-colored sweater, and she looked up and dropped a stitch as they approached.

Madame Perceval smiled. "Pick up your stitch," she said. "We can wait."

Mlle. Duvoisine picked up her stitch, rolled up the knitting, put it into a drawer, and said, "There. Now what can I do for you, Madame Perceval?"

Madame Perceval pushed Flip forward. "This child sounds like a frog with a cold and I thought you'd better have a look at her."

"Open your mouth," Mlle. Duvoisine said to Flip. She peered down her throat, said "hmm," and pulled her thermometer out of her pocket, popping it into Flip's mouth.

Madame Perceval sat on the desk, opened the drawer, and pulled out the sweater. "A work of art," she sighed. "My knitting always looks as though a cat had nested in it."

"My skiing looks as though I had my skis on backwards," Mlle. Duvoisine said. "Radio says snow tonight. What do you think?"

"Smells like it, and it's about time we had some. Fräulein Hauser's been opening the window in the faculty room every ten minutes to sniff the air, and freezing the rest of us to death."

Mlle. Duvoisine drew the thermometer out of Flip's mouth and looked at it. "Well, it's barely ninety-nine, but with that throat and voice I think you'd better come to the infirmary overnight, Philippa. You won't be missing any classes. If your temperature's normal tomorrow, I'll let you up."

"Oh, please!" Flip begged, dismay flooding her face. "Please don't make me go to bed, please! I feel wonderful, just wonderful, really!" Her voice cracked and almost disappeared.

"I knew the infirmary was referred to as the Dungeon," Mlle. Duvoisine said, "but I didn't think it was considered as terrible as all that. Go get your night things and your toothbrush, Philippa."

"But I'm not sick," Flip protested hoarsely.

Mlle. Duvoisine looked at Madame Perceval and raised her eyebrows. "I don't want any more nonsense," she said briskly. "Go get your things and be back here in ten minutes."

Flip opened her mouth to speak again, but Madame Perceval said quietly, "Philippa," and she turned and ran miserably down the corridor.

"Really!" she heard Mlle. Duvoisine exclaim. "Now what's the matter with the child?"

Oh, dear, Flip thought. Now Madame will think I'm sulking again and Paul will think I've broken my word.

And she gathered up her pajamas and toothbrush and trailed miserably back to the infirmary.

When she was in bed with the hot water bottle Mlle. Duvoisine had brought her as a peace offering, she could think of nothing but way after impossible way to let Paul

know why she couldn't come to the château that afternoon.

"You look as though you had something on your
mind, Philippa," Mlle. Duvoisine said when she brought
in the lunch tray.

"I have," Flip answered in the strange raucous voice
that issued in so unwelcome a manner from her throat.
"Please, couldn't I get up, Mademoiselle Duvoisine? I'm
not sick, truly, and I do so hate being in bed."

"What is this nonsense?" Mlle. Duvoisine asked
sharply. "You can hear what you sound like yourself. I
know you aren't ill, but I have you in bed so that you
won't be, and so that you won't give your germs to
anyone else. If you dislike me so intensely that you can't
bear to be around me, just get well as quickly as you can."

"Oh, no. Mademoiselle Duvoisine, it isn't that!" Flip
protested. "It isn't anything to do with you. I just promised someone I'd do something this afternoon, and I
don't know what they'll think if I don't keep my word."

"I can give anyone a message for you, explaining that
you're in the infirmary," Mlle. Duvoisine said, and her
voice was kind.

"I'm afraid you couldn't, to this person," Flip answered mournfully. "Thank you ever so much anyhow,
Mademoiselle Duvoisine, and I'm sorry to be such a
bother."

"All right, Philippa." Mlle. Duvoisine put the lunch
tray down and left.

When she brought in Flip's tea she said, "Since you're
the only victim in my dungeon at present, Philippa, I
think I'll run down to the faculty room for an hour. If
you want me for anything, all you need do is press that
button. It's connected with the faculty room as well as

my desk, and Miss Tulip or I will come right away."

"Thank you very much," Flip said. "I'm sure I won't need anything."

"I've filled your hot water bottle for you," Mademoiselle said kindly and stopped at the window, screwing in the top. "It's just beginning to snow. Now Fräulein Hauser and Madame Perceval and all the skiers will be happy. Sure you don't mind my leaving you?"

"Oh, no, Mademoiselle!"

This was the opportunity Flip had not dared hope for. When Mlle. Duvoisine had left she sprang out of bed and got her clothes out of the closet. She dressed without giving herself time to think. If Mlle. Duvoisine were going to be gone an hour, she would just have time, if she ran, to get to the château, tell Paul what had happened, and get back to the infirmary. That is, as long as she wasn't caught. But she knew that she must not let herself even think about being caught. Desperately she shoved her pillows under the covers so that they looked like someone asleep, peered out the door, saw that the way down the corridor was clear, and pelted for the back stairs. The girls were strictly forbidden to use the back stairs, which afforded a means of entrance and exit that could not be detected by the teacher on duty at the desk in the lounge, but Flip was too desperate to care. When she got out the small back door she looked around wildly and ran for the woods like one pursued. Thank heaven everyone was at tea. When she got in sight of the château she was winded, her knee ached, and her hair was flecked with the first falling flakes of snow. She did not see Paul and her heart sank.

"Paul!" Flip cried, her throat dry, her voice coming out in an ineffectual squeak. "Paul!"

There was no answer. She tried to call again, but this time her voice seemed to have left her completely and only her lips shaped the syllable of Paul's name. Then she heard the familiar baying bark, and Ariel came bounding out of the château to meet her, jumping up at her and knocking her down in his pleasure. She scrambled to her feet, hugging him on the way up, and then she saw Paul come running around a corner of the château.

"What happened to you, Flip!" he cried. "I thought you weren't coming."

"So did I," Flip croaked, "and I can't stay."

"What's the matter with your voice?"

"I have a cold, they've got me in the infirmary, I managed to escape, but I've got to rush back or I'll be caught, I'll come next Saturday unless something awful happens to keep me away." The words came out in one hoarse gasp.

"Flip, you idiot!" Paul cried. "What do you mean by coming here."

"But I said I'd come!" Flip panted. "I've got to get back."

"Not until you rest and get your breath back," Paul commanded. "You'll make yourself really ill."

"But, Paul," Flip wailed, "I've *got* to get back. If Mademoiselle Duvoisine finds out I've gone, I'll be expelled!" Tears rushed to her eyes.

Paul took her hand and shook his head. "Flip, Flip," he said. "Don't you realize what a little idiot you were to make this dangerous trip just to tell me you *couldn't* come? You should know that I understand you well enough to know that if you didn't come you'd have a reason. You should never have gotten out of bed and come all this way through the snow. But"—suddenly his eyes were warm with affection—"it was just like you to do it. Now, go back and take care of yourself."

"I will—good-bye." And she turned back down the mountain.

Flip ran. Going down the mountain was quicker, though not much easier, than coming up had been. Several times she slipped on the wet pine needles and almost fell. The snow was coming more thickly now, and a cloud had folded itself about the school, so that its outlines were lost in gray fuzziness. As she slipped in the small side door she heard someone coming down the back stairs. It was Fräulein Hauser, on her way to the ski room to wax her skis. Flip pressed into the shadows until Fräulein Hauser passed on down the damp corridor and then Flip suddenly wilted against the wall. But every moment that she was away from the infirmary was dangerous; there was no time for her to lean there limply and catch her breath, so she gave herself a shake and hurried up the stairs. She opened the door at the third floor and peered out. The corridor was empty. She held her breath, ran for the infirmary, and opened the door a crack. Mlle. Duvoisine's desk was unoccupied. She made a mad dash for her room, threw off her clothes, dumped them onto the floor of the closet, and scrambled into bed, pushing the pillows out of her way.

She was safe.

She lay in bed, her heart knocking against her chest. Through the window she could see the snow coming down in great soft white petals. The snow clouds in which the school lay obscured everything. She could not see the Dents du Midi or the lake or even the big elm trees that girdled the school. Everything was a soft gray filled with the gently dropping snow.

She was still a little shaky when Mlle. Duvoisine came in. "All right, Philippa?"

"Yes, thank you, Mademoiselle Duvoisine." She hoped the hoarseness would account for the breathlessness of her voice.

Mlle. Duvoisine took her pulse. "Good heavens, child, your pulse is racing," she exclaimed, and took Flip's temperature. But the thermometer registered only ninety-nine. Mlle. Duvoisine put her hand on Flip's forehead and Flip was terrified that the nurse would feel her wet hair, but all she said was, "Have you been asleep? Have you too many covers? You seem to be perspiring."

"I'm very comfortable," Flip told her. "The hot water bottle's lovely. I hope you had a pleasant tea, Mademoiselle."

"Yes. Thanks. Everybody's very pleased about the snow, though Madame Perceval says it's going to stop soon and there won't be enough for skiing."

"In Connecticut where I was born," Flip said, trying to sound casual so that Mlle. Duvoisine would think she had just been lying in the bed all afternoon, "people talk about the first snowfly. I think that's beautiful, don't you? Snowfly."

"Yes, beautiful," Mlle. Duvoisine said. "Think you can eat your supper?"

"Oh, yes," Flip cried hoarsely. "I'm famished." And she was.

Mlle. Dragonet made it a practice to visit the girls in the infirmary, and she came to see Flip that evening, sitting in her erect, stiff manner in the chair Mlle. Duvoisine had drawn up for her. It was the first time Flip had spoken to the principal since the first day of school, and she was very nervous. Mlle. Dragonet held herself aloof from the girls, delegating many duties that would ordinarily have been hers to Madame Perceval, and the bravest of them regarded her with timidity. She conducted a class in seventeenth-century French literature for the seniors; she held morning exercises in the Assembly Hall; and once a week she presided over a faculty table in the dining room. The little visits to the infirmary were more dreaded than anticipated by the girls, and Flip had forgotten all about the prospect in the other excitements of the day until Mlle. Duvoisine announced Mlle. Dragonet's arrival.

"I'm sorry to hear you aren't well, Philippa," the principal said formally.

"Oh, I'm fine, really, thank you, Mademoiselle Dragonet," Flip croaked.

"Mademoiselle Duvoisine tells me you haven't much fever."

"Oh, no, Mademoiselle Dragonet." Flip looked at the principal and realized with a start that she bore a faint family resemblance to her niece. The thin, aristocratic nose was very like Madame Perceval's, and there was a similarity in the shape of the mouth, though Madame Perceval's had a sweetness that Mlle. Dragonet's lacked. But there was the same flash of humor in the eyes, which were the same gold-flecked gray.

As though reading her thoughts, Mlle. Dragonet said, "Madame Perceval tells me your work in her art classes is very promising."

"Oh," Flip breathed.

"Your scholastic record is in general quite satisfactory."

"Oh," Flip said again.

"I hope you are enjoying school?"

Flip knew that Mlle. Dragonet wanted her to say yes, so she answered, "Oh, yes, thank you."

"Are you enjoying the other girls?"

"Oh, yes, thank you."

"Sometimes the Americans find our European girls are younger for their years, less sophisticated."

"Oh," Flip said. "I hadn't noticed."

"You have friends you enjoy?"

Flip hesitated; then she thought of Paul and answered, "Oh, yes, thank you."

Mlle. Dragonet rose, and Flip, with sudden insight, realized that the principal, though so calm and fluent when speaking to a group of girls, was almost as shy as she herself was when confronted with an individual, and these infirmary visits cost her a real effort.

Mlle. Dragonet ran her fingers in a tired fashion over her gray hair. "It has been a long day," she said to Flip, "and now the snow has started and the girls will be happy and we will have numerous strained muscles from overenthusiastic skiers. But as long as the girls are happy, perhaps that is all right. If anything should ever trouble you, remember you have only to come to me."

"Thank you very much, Mademoiselle Dragonet," Flip said. "I'll remember."

Getting to the château was difficult the next Saturday, although Madame Perceval had been right and the snow had stopped and temporarily dashed the skiers' hopes. But enough snow remained on the ground so that Flip put on her spiked boots to help her climb the mountain.

Up above her the mountain had a striped, zebralike look, long streaks of snow alternating with rock or the darker lines of the evergreens. The air was cold and clear and sent the color flying to her cheeks.

Paul greeted her with a relieved shout, crying, "Are you all better, Flip?"

"Oh, yes, I feel fine now."

"I was worried about you. I was afraid you might have caught more cold from coming last Sunday. You shouldn't have, you know."

"I had to," Flip said. "I promised."

"I knew something you couldn't help had kept you. Of course I was a little afraid you'd been caught and they were keeping you from coming. Did you have any trouble getting here today? What will you do when there's a *real* snow, Flip? You'll never be able to make it."

"I'll make it," Flip assured him. "Where's Ariel?"

"He's home with my father. Flip, I—I've done something that may make you angry."

"What?"

"Well, I got to thinking. It's so terribly cold in the château; I'm sure that's why you caught cold, and I didn't think we should go back there in the damp today, so I told my father about you. He won't give us away, Flip, I made him promise."

"Are you sure?" Flip asked anxiously.

"Quite sure. My father would never break his word. Anyhow, he's a philosopher and things like girls' schools and rules and regulations and things don't seem as important to him as they do to other people. He told me to bring you home with me and he said he'd fix some real hot chocolate for us. So come along."

Flip followed Paul over the snow, past the château, and down an overgrown driveway. Grass and weeds and bits of stubble poked up through the snow and it did not look like much of a snowfall here, though the drifts had seemed formidable enough on her way up the mountain from school.

A tall, stooped man, whom Flip recognized as the man she had seen Paul with in the chalet on the Col de Jaman, met them at the door to the lodge. Ariel came bounding out to welcome them noisily.

"My father," Paul announced formally. "Monsieur Georges Laurens. Papa, my friend, Miss Philippa Hunter."

Georges Laurens bowed. "I am happy indeed to meet you, Miss Hunter. Come in by the fire and get warm." He led them into a room, comfortable from the blazing fire in the stone fireplace, and gently pushed Flip into an easy chair. She looked about her. Two beautiful brocades were hung on the walls and there were what seemed like hundreds of books in improvised bookshelves made of packing cases. Two or three lamps were already lit against the early darkness which had settled around the mountainside by this time of the afternoon, and Flip saw a copper saucepan filled with hot chocolate sitting on the hearth.

"Flip's afraid you'll let the cat out of the bag, Papa," Paul said.

Georges Laurens took a long spoon, stirred the chocolate, and poured it out. He handed a cup to Flip and pushed Ariel away from the saucepan. "Watch out, you'll burn your nose again." Then he turned to Flip. "Why should I let the cat out of the bag? You aren't doing anyone any harm and you're giving a great deal of pleasure to my lonely Paul. In fact, I like so much the idea of Paul's having your companionship that my only concern is how to help you continue your visits. As soon as we have a heavy snow you won't be able to climb up the mountains through the woods to us, and in any event someone would be sure to find you out sooner or later and you would be forbidden to come, if nothing else. These are facts we have to face, isn't that so?"

"Yes, that's so," Flip said.

"She has to come," Paul said very firmly.

Georges Laurens took off his heavy steel-rimmed spectacles and wiped them on his handkerchief. Then he took the tongs and placed another log on the fire. "My suggestion is this: Why don't I go to the headmistress of this school and get permission for Miss Flip to come to tea with us every Saturday or Sunday afternoon. That would be allowed, wouldn't it?"

"I don't know," Flip said. "Esmée Bodet's parents are spending a month in Montreux and she has dinner with them every Sunday. But Paul's a boy and we're not allowed to have dates until we're seniors."

"I think if I were very charming"—Georges Laurens refilled her cup with hot chocolate from the copper saucepan—"I could manage your headmistress. What is her name?"

"Mademoiselle Dragonet," Flip told him. "We call her the Dragon," she said, then added, remembering the visit in the infirmary, "but she's really quite human."

Georges Laurens laughed. "Well, I shall be St. George, then, and conquer the dragon. I will brave her in her den this very afternoon.

"And now I suggest that you get back to your school

and tomorrow we will have a proper visit, and I will come for you and bring you over." He held out his hand. "I promise."

It never occurred to Flip that on this last forbidden trip to the château she might be caught. Luck had been her friendly companion in the venture and now that the visits to Paul were about to be approved by authority, surely fortune would not forsake her. But, just as she came to the clearing where the railroad tracks ran through the woods, she saw two figures in warm coats and snow boots and recognized Madame Perceval and Signorina del Rossi. She darted behind a tree, but they had evidently caught a glimpse of her blue uniform coat, for Signorina put a gloved hand on Madame Perceval's arm and said something in a low voice, and Madame Perceval called out sharply, "Who is it?"

Flip thought of making a wild dash for safety, but she knew it would be useless. They were between her and the school and they would be bound to recognize her if she tried to run past them. So she stepped out from behind the tree and confronted them just as a train came around the bend. In a moment the train was between them; she was not sure whether or not they had had an opportunity to recognize her in the misty dark—the school uniforms were all identical and there were dozens of girls with short fair hair. Now was her chance to run and hide. They would never find her in the dark of the woods and the train would give her a good chance to get a head start. But somehow, even if this meant that she would never be given permission to see Paul, she could not run like a coward from Madame Perceval, so she stood very quietly, cold with fear, until the train had passed. Then she crossed the tracks to them.

"Thank you for waiting, Philippa," Madame Perceval said.

She stood, numbly staring at the art teacher, her fingers twisting unhappily inside her mittens.

"Did you know you were out of bounds, Philippa?" Madame Perceval asked her.

She shook her head. "I didn't remember where the bounds were." Then she added, "But I was pretty sure I was out of them."

Signorina stood looking at her with the serene half smile that seldom left her face even when she had to cope with the dullest and most annoying girls in her Italian classes. "Where were you going, little one?"

"Back to school."

"Where from?"

"I was—walking."

"Was it necessary to go out of bounds on your walk?" Madame Perceval asked coldly. "Mademoiselle Dragonet is very severe with girls who cross the railroad tracks."

Flip remembered the walk on which she had first met Ariel, and how, somehow, it had been necessary to go up, up the mountain. "I wanted to climb."

"Were you alone?" Madame Perceval looked at her piercingly, but the dark hid the girl's expression. When she hesitated, Madame pursued, "Did you meet anyone?"

"Yes," Flip answered so low that she could scarcely be heard.

"You'd better come back to the school with me,"

Madame Perceval said. She turned to Signorina. "Go along, Signorina. Tell them I'll come when I can."

In silence Flip followed Madame down the mountain. When she slipped on a piece of ice and her long legs went flying over her head, Madame helped her to pick herself up and brush off the snow, but she said nothing. They left the trees and crossed the lawn, covered with patches of snow, and went into the big hall. Madame Perceval led the way upstairs, and Flip followed her, on up the five flights and down the hall to Madame's own rooms. Madame switched on the lights and when she spoke her voice was suddenly easy and pleasant.

"Sit down, Philippa." Flip's spindly legs seemed to collapse under her like a puppy's as she sat on the stool in front of the fire. "Now," Madame went on. "Can you tell me about it?"

Flip shook her head and stared miserably up at Madame. "No, Madame."

"Who did you go to meet?"

"I'd rather not say. Please."

"Was it anybody from school?"

"No, Madame."

"Did anybody at school have anything to do with it?"

"No, Madame. There wasn't anybody else but me."

"And you can't tell me who it was you went to meet?"

"No. I'm sorry."

"Philippa," Madame said slowly. "I know you've been trying hard and that the going has been rough for you. I understand your need for interests outside the school. But the rules we have here are all for a definite purpose and they were not made to be lightly broken."

"I wasn't breaking them lightly, Madame."

"Once a girl ran away and was killed crossing the railroad tracks. They are dangerous, especially after dark. You see they are placed out of bounds for a very good reason. And if there's anybody you want to see outside school, it's not difficult to get permission. If you were one of the senior girls, I might think you were slipping away to meet one of the boys from the school up the mountain. But I know that's not the case. I don't like having to give penalties, and if you'll tell me about it, I promise you I'll be as lenient as I can."

But Flip's thoughts were rushing around in confusion, and she thought, If I tell now, they'll never give me permission to see Paul.

So she just shook her head while she continued to stare helplessly at the art teacher.

Madame started to speak again, but just then the telephone rang and she went over to it. "Yes? . . . Yes, Signorina!" She listened for a moment, then burst out laughing and continued the conversation in Italian. Flip could tell that she was pleased and rather excited about something. They talked for a long time and Flip could tell that Madame was asking Signorina a great many questions. When she hung up she turned to Flip, and her face was half smiling, half serious. "Philippa," she said, "I know I can trust you."

"Yes, Madame."

"And I want you to prove yourself worthy of my trust. Will you?"

"I'll try, Madame."

"So it's Paul you've been running off to meet," Madame Perceval said with a smile.

Flip jerked erect on her stool. "How did you know!"

Now Madame laughed, a wonderful, friendly laugh

that took Flip and made her part of a secret they were to share together. "Paul's father, Georges Laurens, is my brother-in-law."

Flip's jaw dropped open. "But Madame!" she sputtered. "But Madame!"

Madame laughed and laughed. Finally she said, "I think you and I had better have another little tea party," and she reached for the telephone. "Fräulein Hauser," she said, "I am excusing Philippa Hunter from tea." Then she went into her little kitchen and put the kettle on. When she came back she said, "Signorina and I were on our way over to borrow a book from Georges and have a visit with him and Paul when we bumped into you. Now tell me how you found Paul."

Flip told her about the way Ariel had come jumping out of the undergrowth at her and how he led her to the château and to Paul.

"I see." Madame nodded. "Now tell me what Paul has told you about himself."

"Why—nothing much," Flip said. "I mean, I know his mother's singing in Italy and Monsieur Laurens is writing a book and Paul is going to be a doctor. . . ."

Madame Perceval nodded again. "I see," she repeated thoughtfully. "Now, Philippa, I suppose you realize that you should be penalized. You've been breaking rules right and left. It's a pretty serious situation."

"I know, Madame. Please punish me. I can stand anything as long as I can see Paul again. If I can't see him again I shall die."

"I don't think you'd die, Philippa. And since you're not a senior, you're not allowed to have dates. Not seeing Paul would be automatic before your penalties were even considered."

The color drained from Flip's face and she stared up at Madame Perceval, but she did not move or say anything.

Madame spread cheese on a cracker, handed it absently to Flip, and leaned back in her chair. She held the cheese knife in her hand and suddenly she slapped it against her palm with a decisive motion. "I'm not going to forbid you to see Paul, Philippa," she said, "but you will have to have a penalty and a stiff one, because the fact that it was Paul you were seeing does not lessen the seriousness of your offense, but I'll decide on that tomorrow. In the meantime I want to talk to you about Paul." For a moment Madame Perceval looked probingly at Flip. Then, as though satisfied with what she saw, she continued. "We've been worried about Paul, and I think you can help us."

"Me, Madame?" Flip asked.

"Yes, you. Yes, I think you of all people, Philippa."

"But how, Madame?"

"First of all, simply by seeing him. Signorina told me that Georges was planning to get permission for you to come to the gate house to see Paul once a week. I shall see that you get the permission. And remember, Philippa, that I am doing this for Paul's sake, not yours."

"Yes, Madame. But Madame—"

"But what, Philippa?"

"Monsieur Laurens asked what Mademoiselle Dragonet's name was. Wouldn't he know?"

Madame Perceval laughed. "He was just playing along with Paul. Paul didn't want you to know he had any connection with the school."

"Oh. But—"

"But what, Philippa?"

"Why are you worried about Paul, Madame?"

"I can't tell you that now, Flip. Paul will let you know himself sooner or later. In the meantime, the best way that you can help him is to continue trying to get on with the girls here at school, and to become really happy here. That sounds like rather a tall order to you, doesn't it? But I think you can do it. You'd like to, wouldn't you?"

"Oh, Madame, you know I would. But please—I don't see—how would that help Paul?"

"Perhaps you've discovered already," Madame said, "that Paul has a horror of anything he can label an institution. He knows that you hate *this* institution. Because he respects you, if he could watch you grow to like it here he might be willing to go back to school himself. Georges is tutoring him, but he needs regular schooling. If he really wants to be a doctor he cannot dispense with formal education, and I believe that one day Paul will make a very brilliant doctor. I know this is all very confusing to you, Philippa, but you must trust me as I am trusting you. All I can tell you is that I think you can help Paul and because of this I am willing to disregard the manner in which you have been seeing him up to now and to see that you have official permission to see him in the future." Madame Perceval stood up. "You'd better report to me tomorrow and I'll tell you what your penalties are. I'm afraid this has been a very slim tea for you, Philippa. If you hurry down to the dining room there may be a few scraps left."

"I'm not hungry," Flip said. "Thank you for—for everything, Madame."

Madame put her hand on Flip's shoulder. "I'm very glad this happened to you, Philippa, instead of—say, one of your roommates. Very glad." She was smiling warmly and Flip's heart leaped with joy at this great praise. Madame gave her a little shove. "Run along now," she said.

Flip was ready and waiting in the big hall when Monsieur Laurens came for her the next afternoon. The girls were all curious and rather envious when, in answer to their questions, they learned that Flip had been given special permission to have tea with Madame's nephew, and she felt that her stock had gone up with them.

"My aunt, Pill, it's really a date!" Gloria whistled.

"I bet Pill's never been out with a boy before," Esmée said. "Have you, Pill? Usually the Americans have more dates than the rest of us, but I bet this is Pill's first date. Are you going to let him kiss you, Pill?"

"Don't be silly," Flip said.

"Anyhow, Black and Midnight said it wasn't a date," Sally added. "I bet this nephew's just a child."

Erna whispered to Flip, "Esmée and Sally're just boy crazy. Don't mind them. Personally I think boys are dopes."

At the gate house an hour later, Flip and Paul lay on the great rug in front of the fire and roasted chestnuts while Georges Laurens watched from his chair and Ariel rested his head on his master's knee.

"So you don't like school?" Georges Laurens asked Flip.

"No, sir."

"Why not?"

"I can't seem to fit in. I'm different."

"And I suppose you despise the other girls?" Georges Laurens asked.

Flip looked surprised for a moment, then hesitated, thinking his question over as she opened and ate a chestnut. "No. I don't despise them. I'm just uncomfortable with them," she answered finally, chewing the delicate tender meat and staring at the delicate unicorn in the tapestry on the wall above her. "But you want to be like them anyhow?" Georges Laurens pursued.

She nodded, then added, "I want to be like them and like myself too."

"You think quite a lot of yourself?"

"Oh, no!" She shook her head vehemently. "It isn't that at all. I think I'm—I'm not anything I want to be. It's just that there are certain things outside me and the way I feel about them that I wouldn't want changed. The way I feel about the mountains and the lake. And stars. I love them so very much. And I don't think the others really care about them. I don't think they really see them. And it's the way I feel about things like the mountains and the lake and stars that I wouldn't want changed."

"You want a great deal, my little Flip," Georges Laurens said, gently stroking Ariel's head, "when you want to be exactly like everybody else and yet be different at the same time."

Paul reached for another chestnut and rolled lazily onto his back. "I sympathize with you, Flip. It's horrible to be in an institution. Couldn't you have stayed at home with your parents?"

"I wanted to," Flip said, "but my grandmother's in Connecticut and right now my father's in China, and my mother's dead. I wanted to travel around with Father, but he said he was going to go to all sorts of places I couldn't go, and I couldn't miss school anyhow." Remembering her promise to Madame Perceval she added, "And I don't hate school nearly as much as I used to, Paul. Truly I don't."

"What do you like about it?" Paul asked bluntly.

"Oh, lots of things," Flip said vaguely. "Well—look at all the things you can learn at school you couldn't learn by yourself. I mean not only dull things. Art, for instance. Madame Perceval's taught me all kinds of things in a few months."

"Go on," Paul said.

"And skiing—Fräulein Hauser's going to teach me to ski."

"I know how to ski," Paul said.

Flip tried again. "Well, there's music. They teach us lots about music and that's fun."

"This is the best way to learn about music," Paul said, going to the phonograph and turning it on. "You don't have to be in school to listen to good music."

Flip gave up.

The record on the Victrola was Bach's *Jesu, Joy of Man's Desiring*. It was music that Flip knew and she sat quietly staring into the fire and listening. It was the first time in three years that she had been able to listen to that music. At home in New York in the Christmases of her childhood her mother had played it and played it. The Christmas after her mother's death Flip had found the record broken and was glad. But now she was listening to it with a kind of peace. She looked over at Paul and said softly, "My mother used to love that . . ."

But Paul did not hear. He jumped up and turned off

the record before it had played to the end and said, "Let's go for a walk."

Flip followed him outside. The evening was still and cold and there was a hint of blue-green left in the sky. The stars were beginning to come out. Flip looked up at the first one she saw and made a wish. I wish Paul may always like me. Please, God. Amen. She wished on the star and there was a sudden panic in her mind because the Paul walking beside her was not the Paul with whom she had spent the afternoon. His face in the last light as she glanced at it out of the corner of her eye seemed stern, even angry, and he seemed to be miles and miles away from her. He had withdrawn his companionship and she searched desperately for a way to bring him back to her.

"Paul," she hesitated, then gathered her courage and went on, "do you remember Christmas when you were very little?"

"No," he answered harshly, "I don't remember."

She felt as though he had slapped her. Why wouldn't he remember? She remembered those first Christmases so vividly. Was he just trying to keep her from talking? Had she unwittingly done something to make him angry?

She glanced at him again but his face was unrelenting and she clenched her mittened hands tightly inside her pockets and said over and over to herself, Please, God, please, God, please, God . . .

"I don't remember!" Paul suddenly cried out and abruptly stopped his rapid walking and wheeled about to face her. "I don't remember." His voice was no longer harsh, but he spoke with an intensity that frightened Flip.

She could only ask, "But why, Paul? Why?"

He reached out for her hands and held them so tightly that it hurt. "I don't know why . . . that's the hardest part. I don't remember anything at all beyond the last few years."

Flip tried to make it seem unimportant—to say something, anything, that would make Paul relax. None of this was as serious as he thought—lots of people had poor memories. Anyway it had nothing to do with their friendship. "Paul," she began—but he was not listening. He was not even conscious that she had spoken.

Flip was silent. Paul's tenseness was so tight that even a word might shatter it into something uncontrollable. Whatever was keeping Paul from remembering was something so terrible that it was completely outside her experience.

"I don't want to frighten you," Paul said, "but, Flip, I have to tell you—I don't know who I am."

FOUR
The Lost Boy

Flip did not say anything. She just stood there and let Paul hold her hands too tightly and she felt that somehow the pain in her hands might ease the pain in his mind. Then he dropped her hands and started to walk again, but more slowly. When he began to speak she listened intently, but it was impossible to make it seem real. The story Paul was pouring out to her now was like a movie, or something in a book. The concentration camps. The children and the children's parents gassed and burned. The cold and the hunger, and afterward the lostness. The children roaming and scavenging the streets like hungry wolves.

"I was one of the lucky ones," Paul said in a low voice. "My mother and father found me. I mean—Monsieur and Madame Laurens . . . You'll have to understand, Flip, if I keep calling them my mother and father —but that's the way I think of them now, and I don't remember anyone else for a mother and father."

Flip nodded and Paul continued, his face tense in the starlight. "They found me in a bombed-out cellar in Berlin when my mother was singing there for the troops just after the war was over. I'd been trapped there somehow and I was nearly dead, I guess, but I kept on calling and they found me and rescued me. And for some reason I didn't want to be rescued. It's like sometimes when you try to save an animal he snarls and bites at you before he realizes that you aren't going to hurt him more. A dog was run over on our street once—not Ariel, another dog—and he kept trying to bite at me for a long time until he realized that I wanted to help him. His back was broken and I had to chloroform him. Dr. Bejart helped me." Paul stopped talking and continued to walk so rapidly that Flip almost had to run to keep up with him. She looked up through the bare trees and the last color had drained from the sky and the full flowering of stars was out and they seemed to be caught in the topmost branches of the trees like blossoms. By their light she could see Paul quite clearly, but she knew that she must not say anything to him. They had walked beyond the château now and behind her she could hear an owl calling forlornly from one of the turrets.

"I don't really remember anything before my mother and father found me," Paul said. "Sometimes I remember bits of the concentration camp. Aunt Colette thinks it's because of the concentration camp that I'm afraid of institutions. I might as well admit it, Flip, I am *afraid* of institutions. I think if I could remember I wouldn't be afraid. Sometimes when I'm in the château I feel as though I were going to remember, but I never do. I remember bits of the camp, the way you sometimes remember bits of a nightmare, but when I try really to remember it's like going out of a bright room into a dark room and you can't see anything in the dark except strange shapes and shadows. . . ."

"Oh, Paul," Flip whispered. She could think of no words of comfort or reassurance, so she whispered, "Oh, Paul . . ." again to let him know that she was listening and caring.

"I know your mother's dead," he said, "and that's terrible, but you remember her, don't you?"

She could not say, "Of course," so she nodded, murmuring, "Yes."

"I think my parents have to be dead," Paul said. "I could bear them being dead if only I could remember them. It's like being blind, not remembering. When people talk about the five senses they forget memory. Memory's like a sense . . . Flip, I have never said these things to anyone before. I know my mother and father— the Laurenses—have done everything they possibly could to find out where I come from and who I am. And they love me, and I love them, and I don't want to hurt them by talking to them the way I'm talking to you. You're not like a sister to me. I don't think I'd talk this way to a sister. You're—you're special." He turned abruptly and they started walking back to the gate house. He had forged ahead, but he slowed down and looked back at her. "Any more word from lusting Eunice?"

He had made both of them smile. "I flush her letters down the toilet," Flip said. "I wish I could make Eunice vanish that easily. If she marries my father . . ."

"Don't borrow trouble," Paul said. "Are you cold?"

She shivered, and said, "No."

"You must be cold. You wouldn't be shivering if you weren't. We'll go back and roast some more chestnuts." She walked along beside him and suddenly he turned to her and smiled and his voice was Paul's voice again. "We're going to have wonderful times this winter, Flip!" he said. "When you learn how to ski we can go skiing together. And in the spring we can go for trips on the lake and in the summer we can go swimming. I'm glad you came to the château, Flip."

"Oh!" Flip said. "Supposing I hadn't."

The next afternoon the sky clouded over and it began to snow and it snowed all afternoon and all night and the following afternoon skiing began. Fräulein Hauser met the beginners in the ski room and told them the various parts of the skis and the ski poles and how to take care of them. Flip clutched Eunice's discarded skis and felt happy with the excited kind of anticipation that comes before Christmas. Somehow she knew she would be able to ski and maybe if she turned out to be a really wonderful skier the girls would like her better and then she would begin to like school and she would be better able to help Paul.

But when they got out on the gentle slopes where Fräulein Hauser taught the beginners it wasn't at all the way she had imagined and hoped it would be. Instead of all at once being able to fly over the snow like a bird as she had dreamed, she found that no sooner was she on her feet than she was flat on her back, skis up in the air, or with her head buried in the snow, or doing a kind of wild split. Fräulein Hauser was not unkind, but after a while she said, "You don't seem to have much aptitude for this, do you, Philippa?"

Flip gritted her teeth. "I'll learn."

"I hope so." Fräulein Hauser sounded dubious.

Every afternoon Flip went out grimly with the beginners. She was covered with bruises and every muscle in her body ached, but she was determined that she was going to learn how to ski, that in this one thing at any rate she would not fail. When the other beginners laughed at her tumbles she tried desperately to laugh back, to pretend that she thought it was funny too.

At the end of the ski class on Friday afternoon, Fräulein Hauser called her back to the ski room as the others left.

"I don't want to hurt your feelings, Philippa, but I think you'd better drop skiing. You'll enjoy the ice skating when the hockey field is flooded, I'm sure, and in the meantime there are walks, and gym work."

"But why, please, Fräulein Hauser?" Flip gasped in dismay.

"You just don't seem able to learn, and I'll have to admit I can't teach you. I'm afraid you'll hurt yourself in one of your falls and I think it would be best if you just give it up."

Flip looked at the racks and racks of skis as they suddenly began blurring together. "I'd rather keep on, please, Fräulein Hauser, if it's all right."

"I'm afraid it isn't all right," Fräulein Hauser said impatiently. "I just can't have you in my class. I'll put you on the walk list for tomorrow."

Flip turned her head and left. She walked blindly

down the corridor but she had managed to control her tears by the time she got to the big hall.

On Sunday she could not help telling Paul of her defeat. Paul had immediately seen that something was wrong, asking, "What's the matter?"

"I know I could learn to ski if she'd just let me go on trying," Flip persisted. "I know I could." Ariel was licking her face in a worried manner and she put her head down on his back to try to hide the tears that were threatening.

"Bring your skis over next Sunday and I'll help you," Paul told her.

"Oh, would you really, Paul?"

"I said I would. Do you think it's because of your bad knee you told me about?"

Flip shook her head. "No. My father asked the doctor when Eunice gave me her skis and he said skiing was fine for me. So it isn't that."

"Well, bring your skis next time then," Paul told her.

So Flip brought her skis over. Madame Perceval arrived just as they were about to set off.

"Hello, Philippa, Paul, what's this?" she asked, fending off Ariel's frantic welcome.

"I'm going to teach Flip to ski," Paul announced.

"Oh?"

"Fräulein Hauser said I had to drop skiing," Flip explained.

"Why, Philippa?"

"She said I just couldn't learn and she couldn't teach me. But, Madame, I'm sure I *can* learn, I'm sure I can."

"Why don't I go out with you and Paul," Madame Perceval said, "and we'll see."

She watched while Flip put on her skis, watched her push off, fall down, push off, and fall down again.

"Where did you get your skis?" she asked.

"A friend of my father's gave them to me. They were hers."

"Take them off for a moment," Madame Perceval said. "Now raise your arm." She measured the skis against Flip. "Just as I thought. They're much too long for you. I don't know what your father's friend was thinking of. She can't know much about skiing."

"Well, she says she's skied a lot," Flip said. "Maybe she was trying to impress Father. He doesn't know anything about skiing. He used to use snowshoes when he was a boy."

Madame Perceval took the skis away from Flip. "No wonder you couldn't learn on these. They would be too long for Paul. I don't know why Fräulein Hauser didn't notice it at once."

"She probably would have on anybody else. People just expect me to be bad at sports."

Madame Perceval laughed. "You're probably right, Philippa. And Fräulein Hauser certainly has her hands full with beginners this year. Now, there's a pair of very good skis back at school that would be just about right for you. One of the girls from last year left them. I think I'll run along back and get them. You and Paul wait inside for me."

"Oh, thank you, Madame!" Flip cried.

"Thank you, Aunt Colette," Paul added.

She and Paul went indoors. Georges Laurens was shut

up in his tiny study, deep in concentration, so they did not speak to him, but went over to the fire, stripping off jackets and sweaters. For a moment they were silent and Flip knew that Paul did not want to talk about any of the things he had told her, or to have her talk about them.

"Papa's been writing all day, except when he went to get you," Paul said, talking nervously as he stared into the fire. "I was afraid that he might forget to go for you, but he didn't."

"Thank goodness for that," Flip sighed.

Paul stood up. "I'm hungry. I'll go get us some bread and cheese from Thérèse." He disappeared in the direction of the kitchen and came back with a chunk of cheese, half a loaf of bread, and a bone-handled carving knife. Flip lay on the hearth, using Ariel as a pillow.

"Aunt Colette was over here last night," Paul said, "and that Italian teacher, Signorina what's-her-name."

"Signorina del Rossi."

"That's right," Paul said. "And they were talking about you."

"About me! What did they say?" Flip cried, sitting up.

"Well, I didn't hear all of it because I was reading."

"But what did they say?" Flip asked again.

"Well, Signorina was saying that it was the first time Aunt Colette's ever taken a special interest in any one girl. And Aunt Colette laughed and said that you had great talent and then she said that an artist's life was a hard one but she was afraid you were stuck with it. And then she said—now, don't get angry with me, Flip—"

"Go on."

"Well, she said you were a nice child when you didn't spoil it by being sorry for yourself."

"Oh," Flip said. "Oh." And she lay down again, rubbing her cheek against Ariel's fur.

"Here," Paul said. "Have some more bread and cheese. . . . You aren't angry at me, are you, Flip?"

"No."

"Are you sorry for yourself?"

"Yes. I think I am sometimes—"

"Why?"

"Oh, because I want my mother. And the girls don't like me. Oh, and everything. And I want to be with Father instead of at school. But I don't feel that way so much anymore, Paul. And if I can learn how to ski, it will be wonderful. And I love coming here every weekend. And I'm beginning to like school. Truly I am."

"Why do you keep saying that?" Paul asked, holding the bread against his chest and cutting off another chunk. "You keep saying you like school so much and I don't believe you really do at all."

"I *do*," Flip persisted. "I *don't* hate it the way I used to." And she realized with a start that her words were true. While she didn't actually *like* school, she no longer hated it with the sickening passion of only a few short weeks ago.

"Aunt Colette said something else," Paul went on. "Do you want to hear?"

"Of course."

"She said you reminded her of Denise."

"Who's Denise?"

"Her daughter."

"What!" Flip yelled. "Her *daughter*!"

"Hush. Here she comes. Have some more bread and cheese, Flip," Paul said as Madame Perceval came in carrying a pair of skis.

"Here you are, Philippa." Madame Perceval held the skis up. "Let's try these for size."

Flip scrambled to her feet and Madame Perceval tried them against her. "How are they?" Flip asked eagerly.

"Perfect. Couldn't be better. Put on your things and we'll go out and try them."

As Flip snapped the skis onto her boots Madame Perceval said, "Now don't expect miracles, Philippa. The skis don't make as much difference as all that. Just go very slowly and do as I say."

Madame Perceval was right. Flip was not able, all of a sudden, to ski like an angel because of the new skis. But she no longer fell quite so frequently, or had such a desperate struggle to get to her feet again.

"Better, much better!" Madame Perceval cried as Flip slid down a tiny incline and stopped without falling. "Now turn around."

Flip raised her leg and the long ski no longer tumbled her ignominiously onto the snow. She snapped her other leg around and there she was, all in one piece and erect.

"Bravo!" Madame cried. "Now herringbone up the little hill and come down again."

Her tongue sticking out with eagerness, Flip did as Madame Perceval told her.

"Good," the art teacher said. "Good, Philippa. More spring in your knees if you can. How about that bad knee? Does it bother you?"

"Not much." Flip shook her head. "Oh, Madame, do you think I can learn?"

"I know you can. Just don't stick your tongue out so

far. You might bite it off in one of your tumbles."

"Do you think Fräulein Hauser will take me back in the ski class?"

"Wait! Wait!" Paul cried, waving his ski poles in wild excitement. "I have a much better idea."

Madame laughed and ducked as one of the sticks went flying. "All right, Paul. Calm down and tell us this magnificent idea." But Flip could see that she was pleased because Paul sounded excited and happy, and the dark look had fled from his face.

"Well, Flip was telling me about this ski meet you have at school and how everybody can go in for it and there's a prize for form, and a long race, and a short race, and a prize for the girl who's made the most progress and all sorts of things. And I think it would be wonderful if we could teach Flip and she could enter the ski meet and win and surprise everybody."

Madame Perceval started to laugh, but then she looked at Flip and Paul and their eager, excited faces, and she said slowly, "It would be rather a tall order teaching Flip just on weekends. She needs lots of practice."

"I could slip out in the morning before call over," Flip cried. "If I make my bed before breakfast and hurry breakfast I'd have almost an hour and nobody'd see me then."

"And think how surprised that Fräulein Hauser would be," Paul cried.

"And the girls would be so surprised," Flip shouted. "Erna and Jackie and all of them. Oh, Madame, do you think I could learn? I'd work terribly hard. I'd practice and practice."

"If you keep on improving the way you've improved

this afternoon," Madame Perceval told her, "I'm sure you could."

"Come on, Aunt Colette," Paul cajoled.

Madame Perceval looked at them for a moment longer. Then she smiled and said, "Why not?"

Flip finished her still life of a plaster head of Diana, a wine bottle, a loaf of bread, and a wineglass, early during the next art class.

"That's good, Flip," Madame Perceval said. "Really very good, though your perspective is wobbly—everything's going uphill at quite an alarming angle and poor Diana looks as though she were about to fall on her ear. But the color and texture are excellent. That's really bread, and the transparency of your glass is a great improvement over your last still life. That's good work, Flip."

Flip blushed with pleasure, partly at the praise, and partly because Madame was calling her Flip. Several of the girls looked up at the name and Gloria actually winked at her.

"You have time to start something else," Madame was saying. "Here's a clean sheet of paper and a piece of charcoal. Just draw anything you like. Either from something in the room or from your imagination."

For the past two days Flip had been thinking of three things, Paul, skiing, and Madame's daughter. She had not had another opportunity to ask Paul about Denise, how old she was, or whether she was alive or dead. Somehow Flip felt that she must be dead and that perhaps that accounted for the sadness in Madame Perceval's eyes. She wondered what Madame's daughter would look like and, almost without volition, her hand holding the charcoal moved across the paper and she began to draw a girl, a girl about her own age sitting on a rock and looking out across the valley to the mountains.

The likeness was stronger than she could possibly have guessed. She was trying, more or less, to draw a girl who looked like Madame and who had short hair like hers. But the girl who appeared on the paper did not look like Madame and Flip felt discouraged because she knew the perspective was wrong again and the mountains were too small and far away and the girl's feet weren't right. She sighed and tried to erase the mountains and the feet and correct them.

Madame Perceval stood behind her and looked over her shoulder down at the paper. Flip almost jumped as the art teacher's strong fingers dug into her arm.

"What are you doing?" Madame Perceval's voice was calm and low, but Flip felt the strain in it.

"Just—just a girl looking at the mountains," she stammered. "The—the feet aren't right."

"I'll show you," Madame Perceval said, but instead of explaining what was wrong, and then telling Flip what to do to correct it, as she usually did, she took the charcoal and swiftly put the feet in again herself; and then she took the thumbtacks out of Flip's board and took the paper and walked over to the cupboard with it and Flip saw that her hands were trembling.

In a moment she came back with a fresh piece of paper. "Why don't you try drawing one of the girls in the class?" Madame suggested, and her voice was natural again. "Erna, you've finished, haven't you? Will you sit still and let Flip sketch you?"

"Yes, Madame. How do you want me to sit, Pi—
Philippa—uh—Flip?"

Madame Perceval smiled as Erna stumbled over
Flip's name, and Flip said, "Oh, the way you are now,
looking over the back of your chair is fine, if you're
comfortable."

She took up the charcoal and sketched quickly and
then she laughed because the girl on her paper was so
out of proportion and funny-looking and at the same
time she *was* Erna. In trying to get a likeness, Flip had
over-accentuated and the braces on Erna's teeth were
ridiculous and her chin jutted out and the barrette pulled
the hair back far too tightly from the forehead.

"What are you laughing at?" Erna demanded.

Flip looked at her drawing and thought, Oh, dear,
now Erna will be mad.

But Madame Perceval had come over and was laughing, too, and showing the paper with Erna on it to the
class, and everybody was laughing.

"I think you have a flair for caricature, Flip," Madame said.

And Jackie bounced up and down on her chair, crying, "Draw me, Flip, draw me!"

"Hold still then, Jackie," Madame said, handing Flip
another sheet of paper.

Flip's hand holding the charcoal made Jackie's curly
hair fly wildly about the paper; the enormous, long-
lashed black eyes took up half the page, and the mouth
was a tiny bud above the pointed little chin. Erna had
been watching and as Flip laid down the charcoal for
a moment she grabbed the paper and held it up, shouting, "Look at Jackie! She looks just like a cat!"

"Draw me! Draw me!" All the girls were shouting at

Flip until Madame Perceval stopped them, saying, "Not now, girls. The bell just rang. You can get Flip to draw you anytime. I know she'd like to, wouldn't you, Flip?"

"Oh, yes, Madame!"

So they besieged Flip in the common room with requests for caricatures to send home, and Flip went to her locker, her face bright with happiness, to get her sketch book and pencils.

"Don't make my nose *too* big!" "Should I take my glasses off, Flip?" "Oh, Pill, don't put in my freckles!" "Flip" and "Pill" came indiscriminately, and somehow quite suddenly and surprisingly Flip knew that she no longer minded the "Pill" because it sounded friendly; it was being said to her, not at her.

I'm liking school, she thought. I'm liking it. Now it will sound better when I tell Paul I like it.

Only Esmée Bodet was discontent with her picture. "I don't look like that!" she said, and tore the page across, tossing the pieces into the wastepaper basket.

"She looks exactly like that," Erna said in Flip's ear. "Come on up on the billiard table and let's play jacks." The entire school had a jacks craze on. Even the seniors were playing, though Esmée turned up her nose and said it was a child's game, and continued to play very bad bridge.

"Oh, jacks! Let me play too!" Gloria cried, clambering up and sitting cross-legged on the green felt of the billiard table; and Flip realized that one reason Gloria never lacked for partners, or a place in the common room games, was that she never hesitated to ask.

"Come on, Jackie," Erna called. "Climb up."

Flip was quite good at jacks and Gloria bounced up and down impatiently. "Come on, Pill, miss, can't you? I want a turn." And she gave Flip's elbow a jog, but Flip caught the ball and laughed triumphantly.

"Good for you, Flip," Erna cried. "You can't play if you're going to cheat, Glo."

"It's Erna's turn next, anyhow," Jackie said. "By the way, Pill, I think it's a dirty shame Hauser made you drop skiing."

"Me too." Erna nodded so violently that her hair came out of the barrette and she had to fasten it again.

Flip thought of the progress she had already made on her skis, and smiled to herself. Then she shrugged. "Well, if she thinks I'm too impossible to teach, I guess that's that."

"The mangy old minge," Gloria muttered. "I say, Pill. What're you going to be when you get out of this place, an artist?"

Flip nodded. "I'd like to be. The way my father is. I'd like to paint portraits and do illustrations for children's books." She reached wildly for the jacks ball, which was this time an old golf ball Gloria's mother had sent, but it bounced off the table and Erna scrambled after it.

"At last," she said, bringing it back and collecting the jacks. "I'm going to be a doctor like *my* father. I think it must be wonderful to cut people up and put them back together again." Underneath her joking words Flip could tell that she was serious.

"The trouble is that you can't always put them back together again," Jackie said.

"I will." Erna swept up her jacks with a confident gesture. "If people have their legs and things blown off, I'll discover a way to put them back or give them new ones off dead people."

Flip started to tell Erna that Paul wanted to be a

doctor too, but Gloria, who didn't mind when she herself talked about glass eyes or false teeth, put her hands over her ears. "Oh, stop! Stop!"

"Well, dead people can give their eyes so blind people can see," Erna said, "so I don't see why they shouldn't give their legs and things too."

Gloria clapped her hand over Erna's mouth. "You go talk about your old operations somewhere else."

"Who asked you to play jacks anyhow?" Erna mumbled from behind Gloria's hand. "Let go and let me play. I'm on fivesies, eggs in the basket."

"Foursies."

"Fivesies."

"It's fivesies," Flip corroborated. "Are you going to be a movie actress, Jackie?"

Jackie laughed and waved her arms. "My father says I'll be an actress over his dead body. I haven't thought about it much. Maybe I'll just be a wife like my mother. She says that's a career in itself, only lots of people forget it."

"Love," Gloria sighed, "that's what I'm cut out for."

"Do you believe in love at first sight?" Flip asked and blushed.

"I believe in love." Gloria placed her hand dramatically over her heart. "It's love that makes the world go round."

"Have you seen Maggie Campbell's brother?" Jackie asked. "He's the handsomest man I ever saw. Maggie's going to give me a snapshot of him for Christmas."

Flip sat with her legs stuck out in front of her on the old hotel billiard table, because her stiff knee kept her from sitting cross-legged or on her heels, and watched, and listened, and occasionally said a word, and she felt so excited that she could feel the excitement like hunger in the pit of her stomach. She was excited because for the first time she felt on the inside, and underneath the new warm sense of being one of them was the glorious secret knowledge of Paul—and tomorrow she would see him again.

The first thing Paul asked Flip the next day was, "Have you been practicing your skiing?"

Flip nodded. "Every morning."

"How's it going?"

"Better."

"Well, come on and let's go. Is Aunt Colette coming over?"

"I don't know."

"Well, come on, Flip," Paul said impatiently. "I want to see how much you've improved."

They went out, Ariel rushing madly about them, digging up the snow, running and jumping against them, until Paul had to send him in.

Paul was visibly impressed with Flip's progress, and when Madame Perceval appeared on skis, Paul flew over to her in great excitement. "Flip's a natural born skier, Aunt Colette!" he cried. "She's magnificent!"

Madame Perceval smiled at Paul and held out her hand to Flip. "Let's see what you've accomplished, little one."

She, too, was impressed. "You must have been working hard!" she said.

"Oh, Madame, do you really think so?"

"Just keep up the practicing, Flip, as you've been doing, and I'm sure you'll do fine."

"She'll be quite a shock to everybody at the ski meet, won't she?" Paul asked.

Madame laughed. "She certainly will."

And Flip went to bed that night to dream of soaring through the air on her skis, watched by admiring throngs of girls; of executing the delicate loops of telemarks; and when she woke up in the morning her mind was still a happy jumble of snow conditions and stems.

Flip had thought as she slipped out the ski room door after breakfast each morning that the girls would become curious about her hurried breakfasts and ask what she was doing; but they were used to her disappearances and absences and were too hungry and sleepy and hurried in the cold dark of the mornings to pay much attention to anything besides getting themselves out of their warm beds and then eating as much porridge and rolls and jam as possible with their hot chocolate.

Flip was out practicing intently one Saturday morning when she noticed someone watching her. She looked up, fearful that she was being discovered, but it was no one from the school. It was a man with a dark, wild face, and the look in his eyes frightened her; but he waved and grinned at her cheerfully and moved away. He wore climbing boots and carried a stick and he struck off up the mountain, walking very rapidly. She watched after him until he was lost in the trees, wondering what a strange man was doing on the grounds of a girls' school. Then she thought he might be a new gardener or perhaps someone to help with flooding the hockey field for ice skating, though that was not to be done till the Christmas holidays.

Oh, well, she thought, there's never anybody around who isn't meant to be around, so I guess it's all right.

And she kept on working at the skiing until time to get the mail before call over.

Most of the girls were already at the desk in the hall when she arrived, flushed from her early morning exercise, and Signorina, who was on duty, was giving out the mail. Since she had begun noticing other people besides herself, Flip had learned a lot from the mail. Hardly a day went by that Jackie did not have a letter from her mother. Erna always came rushing eagerly to the desk but seldom received anything. Gloria frequently didn't even bother to come and if she had a letter someone took it to her. Esmée had already begun to get letters from boys and read them aloud to anyone who would listen. Solvei's letters came as regularly as Jackie's, and Sally received hers every Wednesday and Saturday. Eunice's letters, on gray stationery with green ink, usually came on Thursday. From the point of view of the other girls, at least Flip was getting regular mail, but Eunice always said something that galled her.

"Philippa Hunter," Signorina called.

It was not from Eunice. Flip took the letter from her father and opened it eagerly. There was one sheet of writing, and no sketches. Something was wrong.

"My darling baby," he said, beginning the letter as he had not done in years.

Here I am in a hospital in Shanghai, as yellow as any banana. Don't be worried—it's not the bad kind of jaundice, I'm promised, but it's a great nuisance because I have to stay here in bed and rest. It's a horrid nuisance because the doctor says I won't possibly be able to get to you for your Christmas holidays. Flippet, Flippet, don't be too terribly disappointed and don't weep that sweet face into a pulp. Eunice will be delighted to have you for your holidays, and she is in Nice, and the weather will be wonderful, and I know she'll do everything she can to make you happy. Your letters have sounded so much more contented recently and I feel that you are growing up and that you try to enjoy yourself without your yellow old father. I expect to be in Germany and Switzerland shortly after New Year and I promise you that *nothing* will interfere with our Easter.

Flip's disappointment was so acute and overwhelming that she thought for a moment she was going to be sick. She turned and ran until she reached the bathroom and then she shut herself in and leaned against the door and she felt all hollow inside herself, from the top of her head down to her toes, and there was no room in this cold vacuum for tears.

After a few moments she heard a knock. She clenched her fists and held her breath but whoever it was did not go away, and the knock came again. If it's Miss Tulip I'll kick her, she thought in fury.

Then Erna's voice came. "Flip."

"What?" Flip said, sounding hard and forbidding.

"Flip, it's just me. Erna."

"Oh."

"Did you—was it—was there bad news in your letter?"

"No. It's all right." Flip's voice was stifled.

"Well, look, Flip," Erna said. "I just meant . . . Percy's taking call over this morning and you know how strict she is . . . and the bell's about to ring . . ."

Flip opened the door and came out. "Thanks, Erna."

"Oh, that's all right," Erna said uncomfortably. "I'm sorry if it was bad news in your letter."

"It's just that my father's sick in China and I can't be with him for the Christmas holidays," Flip started to explain in a controlled voice. Then she burst out, "And I have to spend the holidays with Eunice—she's a friend of my father's—and I don't like her and if she marries my father I'll—I'll want to kill her."

"Ach, that's awful," Erna said. "I'm awful sorry, Flip. It certainly is awful."

"Well . . ." Flip's voice trailed off, then she spoke briskly. "We'd better get down to call over."

The next day she told Paul about the letter, and for the first time since she had received it she started to cry. Ariel, distressed at her unhappiness, jumped up at her, almost knocking her over, and licked excitedly at her face.

"That Eunice," Paul said, frowning heavily and pushing Ariel away from Flip and sending him over to the hearth. Then he jumped up. "Put on your skis and go on out and start practicing," he commanded. "I'll be out in a minute." And he half-shoved Flip out the door.

Flip went out obediently and put on her skis and started working on her turns. In just a few minutes Paul came flying out of the lodge, shouting, "Flip! Flip!"

He rushed up, panting, and gasped, "My father says you may stay here with us for Christmas if your father says it's all right! And Aunt Colette is going to be with us because my mother can't come." His face was radiant with pleasure.

Flip sat down in the snow, her feet going every which way.

"And you can work on your skiing every day. And I'm sure Aunt Colette can take us up to Gstaad to ski, and to Caux too, so you'll be familiar with Gstaad and all the runs for the ski meet and maybe you will become such a good skier that we can do a double jump! Papa said he'd write your father right away this afternoon. Oh, Flip, it will be wonderful to have you here all the time instead of just on Sunday afternoons!"

"Oh, Paul!" Flip cried and scrambled to her feet. "Oh, Paul! Next to being with Father it's the most wonderful thing in the world. I know he'll let me!"

"Well," Paul said, giving her a quick, shy hug. "What a relief. Come on. Let's get to work on your skiing."

Flip had been skiing conscientiously for about an hour under Paul's tutelage when Madame Perceval came out and called them.

"Come on in to tea, children!"

They skied over to her, Flip with almost as great ease and confidence as Paul, shouting, "Hello, Madame!" "Hello, Aunt Colette!"

"So," Madame said, raising Flip's chin and looking into her eyes. "You're happy about your holidays now?"

"Oh, yes, Madame!"

"I was wondering what had happened to upset you, my problem child. You seemed so much happier and then gloom descended. But you did have some reason this time. It's hard to be away from your father at Christmastime."

"And it would have been awful to be with Eunice," Flip said. "Eunice always makes me feel—well, even clumsier and gawkier and tongue-tieder and everything than I am. But, oh, Madame, I'll love being here, and I'll try to help and not be a bother."

"Hurry up, Flip, take off your skis," Paul called impatiently. "Papa went over to Lausanne to the dentist yesterday and brought us back cakes from Nyffeneggers."

When they had finished tea Madame said, "How about skiing back to school with me, Flip? Feel up to it?"

"Yes, Madame, I think so."

"You haven't skied any distance at all, yet, and I think it would be good for you. Not afraid of skiing in the dark? I'll keep right beside you."

"I'm not afraid, Madame."

They pushed off, Flip feeling excited and happy as she turned around to wave good-bye to Paul, who was standing in the lighted doorway. And Flip thought how beautiful the night was with the stars just coming out, and the pine trees' noble arms bowed with snow, and the shadows of the ruined château looming behind them, and the warmth and comfort of the lodge, the golden light pouring out the open door and Paul standing there waving good-bye.

"Yes," Madame Perceval said, as if in answer to her thoughts. "It's beautiful, isn't it? In the spring the fields are as white as they are now, with narcissi, not snow. . . . Shall we go?"

They started off down the mountainside, Madame calling Flip from time to time to check her speed or give her instructions. Now at last Flip had the feeling of being a bird, of having wings. And as she pushed through the cold night air she felt that it was as solid and entire an element as water. A bird must know this solidity; but as she felt the air against her body the only thing

within her own knowledge with which she could com-
pare it was water, and she felt as she broke through it
that she must be leaving a wake of air behind her, as a
boat does, cutting through water.

Madame let her go faster and faster, and, exhilarated
by the speed and the beauty, she would have gone flying
past the school gates if Madame had not checked her.
They turned through the gates together and moved
slowly down the white driveway.

"That was good skiing, Flip," Madame said. "I'm really very proud of you."

Flip dropped her head in quick confusion, then looked
up with eyes that shone in the starlight. "I love it, Madame, I just love it!"

"You know," Madame told her, "we're not going to
be able to enter you in the beginners' class at the ski
meet. You'll have to go in the intermediate. If you go on
improving at this rate, you'd be disqualified from the
beginners' class. And with all the skiing you'll be able to
do during the holidays I don't think there's any question
but you'll go on improving. I want to work with you on
your left stem turn. Your right is fine, but the left is the
only place where your weak knee seems to bother you.
Don't worry, though. I think a little extra practice and
the left stem will be as good as the right."

They went indoors and Flip put her skis on the rack,
stroking them lovingly. The smell of the ski room, of hot
wax and melted snow and damp wool from the ski
clothes, was almost as pleasant to her now as the smell
of the art studio.

"Madame," she said softly, "thank you so much for
the skis."

"The girl who left them was rolling in money," Madame spoke shortly, "and I suspect it was black market money. They're in far better hands now—or rather on far better feet." She laughed. "Run along upstairs to the common room. There's about half an hour before dinner. We made better time than I expected."

Flip ran up the stairs and across the hall, almost bumping into Miss Tulip.

"Really, Philippa Hunter!" Miss Tulip exclaimed in annoyance. "Will you kindly remember that you are supposed to walk, not run. You used to be such a nice, quiet girl and you're turning into a regular little hoyden." And Miss Tulip shut herself up in the cage of the faculty elevator and pressed the button.

Instead of being crushed by Miss Tulip's irritation Flip had to suppress a laugh as she watched the elevator rise and saw the matron's feet in their long, narrow white shoes slowly disappearing up the elevator shaft. Then, completely forgetting her admonition, she ran on down the corridor and into the common room.

She had just started a letter to her father when the big glass door was opened and Martha Downs and Kaatje van Leyden came in. A sudden hush came over the common room because the senior girls had studies and a special living room of their own on the second floor, and seldom came downstairs unless it was to lecture one of the girls for some misdeed that affected the two school teams, the Odds and the Evens, or that came under the jurisdiction of the student government. Martha and Kaatje walked toward Flip now and she knew that everybody was wondering,   Now what has Pill done?

But Martha smiled in a friendly way and said, "Hi, Philippa."

"Hi," Flip said, standing up awkwardly.

"I hear you're good at drawing people."

"Oh, just sort of caricatures," Flip mumbled.

Erna, who had been listening curiously, broke in. "She's wonderful, Martha! I'll show you the ones she did of Jackie and Gloria and me in the dormitory last night."

Erna had forgotten that they weren't supposed to have books or drawing materials in the dormitory at night, but Martha and Kaatje kindly ignored this and looked at the slips of paper Erna held out. They both laughed.

"Why, you're a genius, Philippa," Kaatje cried.

And Martha said, "We came down to see if you'd do us."

"Oh, I'd love to," Flip said. "Right now?"

"How long does it take you?"

"About a second," Erna told them. "Here's a chair, Martha, and one for you, Kaatje. Run get your sketch book, Flip."

Flip got her pad and a couple of sharp pencils out of her locker. "Just stay the way you are, please," she said to Martha. "That's fine."

It wasn't quite as easy to draw Martha as it had been the girls she saw constantly in the common room and the classroom, or as easy as the faculty, whose caricatures, sketched hurriedly at the end of study halls, had thrown the girls into fits of laughter, but she managed to get a passable exaggeration of Martha's almost Hollywood beauty onto the paper, and the head girl was very pleased.

While Flip was drawing Kaatje, Martha said, "My mother writes me you're going to be spending the holidays in Nice with Mrs. Jackman, Philippa. We're going to be there for a week, so maybe we'll see you."

Flip shook her head, glancing up briefly from her sketch of Kaatje. "I'm not going to be with Mrs. Jackman. I'm staying up the mountain with Paul Laurens."

"Percy's nephew?" Martha asked in surprise. "How did you get to know him?"

"She has tea with him every Sunday afternoon." Erna, who had evidently appointed herself as Flip's spokesman, told the seniors. "She's just come back from there now, haven't you, Flip?"

Flip nodded, tore off her page, and gave it to Kaatje.

"Thanks simply ages, Philippa," Kaatje said. "You'll probably be besieged by every girl in school."

"I don't mind," Flip said. "It's what I love to do. If those aren't right or if you want any more, I'd love to try again."

"We may take you up on that." Martha smiled at her. "Sorry you aren't going to be in Nice for the holidays."

"Flip, you're made," Erna said when the older girls had left. "If Martha and Kaatje like your pictures, there won't be a girl in school who won't want one. I bet you'll get artist's cramp or something."

"It's all right with me." Flip grinned happily.

"And it's wonderful about the holidays. When did that happen?"

"This afternoon. And Madame's going to be there too."

"Percy?" Erna looked dubious. "I'm not sure I'd like that. She's so strict."

"She's not a bit strict when you're not at school. She's

—oh, she's so much fun and she doesn't act a bit like a teacher. And Paul says she'll take us on all kinds of trips on the holidays, to Gstaad, and we'll come down from Caux on a bobsled, and we'll go to Montreux and places to the movies and all sorts of things."

"It's too bad you can't ski," Erna said. And Flip turned away to hide a grin.

FIVE
The Stranger

Flip was out practicing by herself before breakfast several mornings later when she saw the strange man again. At first she did not notice him, and then she became vaguely aware through her concentration on her skiing that someone was watching her, and she swung around and there he was leaning against a tree. This time he did not smile and wave and move away up the mountain. He just stood there watching her and she stared nervously back. He was very thin and his cheeks were sunken and his jaw dark, as though he needed to shave. He wore shabby ski clothes and a small beret and his eyes were very dark and brilliant. She stood, leaning lightly on her ski poles, looking back at him and wishing he would go away, when suddenly he came stumbling across the snow toward her. She started to push away on her skis,

but he made a sudden leap at her and she fell headlong.
She started to scream, but he clapped his hand across
her mouth.

"Don't be afraid. Don't be afraid. I won't hurt you," he
kept saying, and he righted her and stood her up again,
keeping a firm grip on her arm. She could feel each of
his fingers pressing through her sweater and ski jacket
and they hurt as they dug into her arm.

"Let go!" she gasped. "Let me go!"

"It's all right," he repeated. "I won't hurt you. Don't
be afraid."

"But you *are* hurting me! Let go!"

Slowly his fingers relaxed, though he did not release
her. "I didn't mean to knock you down like that. I lost
my balance and fell against you. I'm very tired and hungry. Have you any food?"

She shook her head.

"Just a cracker or a piece of chocolate? Schoolgirls
always have something to eat in their pockets."

She shook her head again. "I haven't anything. What
are you doing here?"

"I'm the—uh—I'm the new janitor. I'm going to keep
the furnace going so you'll be warm enough all winter. I
live—uh—I live up the mountain and I didn't have a
chance to eat breakfast this morning because I overslept.
Are you sure you haven't even a crust of bread?"

"I haven't anything. Won't the cook give you something in the kitchen?"

"She's in a bad mood this morning. What are you
doing out here all alone? Shouldn't you be in the
school?"

"Not till call over at a quarter to nine."

"But why are you here all alone?" the man asked her,

and she was afraid of the hungry look in his dark eyes.

"I'm skiing."

"But why do you ski here all alone every morning?" he persisted.

"I like it."

Now at last he let go of her arm. "Well, I'm off up the mountain," he said, and without another word or a backward glance he struck off across the snow.

The thought of him troubled her until she went in to get the mail before call over. Then she had a letter that made her so angry that she forgot all about him. The letter was from Eunice, and it said:

> My dear Philippa,
>
> I am glad to hear from your father that at last you are getting along better at school. But I must admit that I am rather hurt that you choose to spend the holidays with some strange boy you have just met rather than with me. However, you have always been an odd child, so I suppose I shouldn't be surprised. I do want to say, though, Philippa, dear, that I know your poor father would be happier if you came to Nice, and I assure you that I would see that you had a pleasant vacation. As I said in my letter to you last week, there will be a number of charming young people nearby, and I am sure it would do you good to know them. Just remember that all you have to do if you change your mind is to let me know, and don't forget that you have your father's peace of mind to think of as well as your own choice. It is very hard on him to be laid up in the hospital, poor darling, and I shouldn't think you'd want in any way to add to his

worries. I'm afraid this will make you angry, Philippa, dear, but do remember that I'm just thinking of your best interests and that I'm very fond of you and devoted to your father.

Affectionately, Eunice

Quivering with rage, she tore the letter into as small pieces as possible. Madame Perceval, on duty behind the desk, finished distributing the mail and asked with a smile, "What's the cause of your fury, Flip?"

"It's that Eunice again," Flip said. "A woman who's always after my father. She thinks I ought to spend the holidays with her and I'm afraid she'll try to convince Father that I ought to too. There isn't time for that, is there?"

"No, Flip, there isn't. Anyhow, Mademoiselle Dragonet had a cable from your father this morning giving his permission for you to stay with Paul. She supplanted Georges's cable with one of her own, saying that she thought it far better for you to stay with her nephew than for you to make the difficult trip to Nice. So I don't think you need worry."

"Thank goodness," Flip said. "I think I'd die if I couldn't spend the holidays with Paul. I just wish Eunice hadn't written the letter and tried to spoil things for me."

"Just forget it and enjoy yourself," Madame Perceval advised.

"I will," Flip said, and she ran upstairs to throw the scraps of Eunice's letter in the classroom wastepaper basket; Eunice had used such heavy paper she was afraid it would clog the toilet. Erna was in the classroom before her, sitting glumly at her desk.

"What's the matter, Erna?" Flip asked shyly.

"I can't spend the holidays with Jackie," Erna answered and put her head down on her arms.

Flip perched awkwardly on her desk and put her feet on the chair. "Oh, Erna, why not?"

"My mother wrote Mademoiselle Dragonet and said she wanted me home for Christmas. She doesn't want me home at all. She sent me away to school because she didn't want me home."

"Oh, Erna," Flip said, her voice warm with sympathy.

"Both my brothers were killed in the war," Erna said in a muffled voice. "And I know Mutti wishes it had been me. She always liked my brothers better. I was the baby and so much younger and I always got in the way."

"Oh, no, Erna," Flip protested. "Your mother wouldn't feel like that."

"She does," Erna said. "If my father would be home and be all funny and nice the way he used to be before the war when I was tiny, it would be all right. But he's always at the hospital. He says the only thing he can do to help people's souls is to try to give them strong, well bodies for the souls to grow in, and most of the time he sleeps in the hospital. I think he likes me and I think he's glad because I want to be a doctor, too, but Mutti doesn't like me to be around because I laugh or sing or make noise and that disturbs her unhappiness."

"Oh, Erna," Flip whispered again.

"I don't want to go home," Erna said. "I thought it was going to be so wonderful to be with Jackie. Her mother tells wonderful stories and she wrote me the most wonderful letter, saying how much she would love to have me for the holidays and she wrote my mother and the Dragon saying she'd take good care of me and everything and we were going to go to the theater to see a play and to the opera, but my mother wrote the Dragon and said I couldn't and the Dragon called me to her living room after breakfast and told me. I don't want to go home."

The night before, Flip had heard Maggie Campbell talking to Solvei Krogstad in the common room and almost crying because she was going to have to stay at the school during the holidays, but Erna was continuing. "If I could stay at school it wouldn't be so bad, it would be all right. Lots of girls stay at school. Gloria's going to stay, and Sally, because her parents have gone back to the United States, and lots of them are going to stay. The Dragon takes a chalet at Gstaad for the holidays and Sally stayed last year and said it was wonderful. I love school. I just love it. I wish I could stay here always."

Flip sat quietly on her desk and let Erna talk. This miserable girl was very unlike the brash gamin she was used to, and she ached with sympathy. "I'm sorry, Erna, I'm awful sorry," she said softly.

Erna took a tight ball of a handkerchief out of her blazer pocket and dabbed at her eyes. "Don't tell Jackie I almost cried."

"I won't."

"Sometimes I dream my mother is like Jackie's mother," Erna said, "and comes in and looks at me after I'm in bed to see that I'm covered, and comes in and kisses me in the morning to wake me up. Was your mother like that, Flip?"

Flip nodded.

"It must have been awful when she died."

Flip nodded again.

"I don't think Gloria's mother loves her too much,

but Glo doesn't seem to care. Well, it must be almost time for call over. Come on. We'd better go down and get in line. The holidays won't last too long and then I can come back to school." Erna gave her desk lid a slam and walked briskly to the door.

While she was brushing her teeth that night Flip thought more about Erna. It somehow had never occurred to her that anyone could really love the school. She herself was learning not to hate it, and was beginning to have fun, and to lose some of the dreadful shyness that had tormented her, but she hadn't even thought of really loving school so that she would be miserable whenever she had to leave. She felt a sense of warm companionship with Erna, now that each had witnessed and tried to comfort the other's unhappiness.

When she got back to the room Erna was already in bed, rubbing mentholatum on her chapped hands, Gloria was combing the snarls out of her hair, and Jackie was wrapping a towel around her hot water bottle.

"Hi, Pill," Jackie greeted her. "We've been wondering something."

Flip hardly noticed anymore whether they called her Flip or Pill. When Jackie said "Pill," it sounded like an affectionate nickname, not a term of contempt, and only Esmée continued to use it in a derogatory manner. "What have you been wondering?" she asked.

"Well, you've been seeing Percy every Sunday for a while now. Have you learned anything about her private life?"

"Jackie has a crush on Percy, Jackie has a crush on Percy," Gloria droned.

"If you want to call it that," Jackie said. "I admire her more than anybody in the world except my mother and I'm not ashamed of it."

"Needn't get huffy, ducky." Gloria threw her comb down in disgust and tried to get her snarls out with her fingers. "I must need a new perm. My hair's just awful. It's the way Black and Midnight washes it with that beastly old soap. I'm just as curious about Percy as you are. Where do you suppose *Mr.* Percy is? Come on, Pill. You must have found out something."

"I haven't," Flip said. "Not a thing. Nobody's ever said anything about her husband." She thought of Denise, but said nothing.

"Couldn't you ask?" Gloria rubbed some lip balm over her lips as though it were lipstick.

"Good heavens, no!" Flip cried, aghast.

"Of course she couldn't ask," Jackie exclaimed. "What are you thinking of, Glo?"

"Well, I'd ask if I wanted to know."

"Oh, yes, you would!"

"Well, I would!"

"Well, maybe *you* would," Erna said, "but Flip wouldn't, and neither would I."

This would have crushed Flip, but Gloria merely took her nail scissors out of the manicure box her mother's Emile had sent her for her birthday, and started to clip her toenails.

"Sometimes when Percy thinks no one is looking at her she gets the saddest look in her eyes," Jackie said. "It's as if she hurt deep inside."

"Maybe her husband died on her wedding night and she's mourned for him ever since," Erna suggested.

"Gee, I wish I could put nail polish on my toenails,"

Gloria sighed, "but Black and Midnight would spot it somehow. Maybe he was killed in the war."

"Switzerland wasn't in the war, dopey," Erna said.

"Well, maybe he was French or something, dopey," Gloria retorted. "Or maybe he ran away and left her."

"Hah," Jackie snorted. "I bet if anybody left anybody, Percy would do the leaving."

"Well, maybe he was an awful drunkard and she left him. I bet she's divorced."

"She wears a wedding ring," Jackie said. "She wouldn't wear her wedding ring if she were divorced."

"Well, maybe he has amnesia and he's just wandering about."

Jackie snorted again, then said, "I used to think that when she went out every Sunday afternoon maybe he had T.B. or was insane or something and in a sanitarium and she went to see him. But now we know she just goes to see this Paul." The bell rang and Jackie tucked her hot water bottle carefully under the covers and got in after it.

Lying in bed after Miss Tulip had turned out the lights, and after she had said her prayers, Flip, too, wondered about Madame Perceval. Often she had noticed the sad look in her eyes and thought perhaps it had something to do with Denise. Why is it, she wondered, that things that hurt people make them deeper and more understanding? She was closer to Erna because of the German girl's pain than she had ever been before. Gloria had had bad things happen to her, but they seemed to slide off without touching her. Whatever had happened to hurt Madame Perceval had strengthened her, inwardly, outwardly. Madame Perceval, Philippa realized, had a zest for living that was enlarged rather than diminished by whatever had happened to her husband and daughter.

Am I growing because of Mother? she asked herself. Is it making Father grow? I would like to grow up to be as strong as Madame Perceval.

Then she slid into sleep, and dreamed that she was running to meet her mother down a long path, and just as she got up to her, laughing with delight, her mother turned into Eunice Jackman, who was saying, "Really, Philippa, you're too clumsy for words. Can't you get out of my way?"

Flip saw the dark man once again on the Sunday before the holidays. She was at the gate house and Paul had sent her out to the kitchen to ask Thérèse for some bread and jam. When she opened the kitchen door, there he was leaning against the sink and drinking a cup of coffee. As Flip pushed open the door he put the cup down quickly and slipped out.

"What do you want?" Thérèse asked crossly.

"Some bread and jam, please, Thérèse."

Thérèse gave her the bread and jam and when Flip got back to the living room she asked Paul, "Who is that man?"

"What man?"

"I don't know. There was a man in the kitchen drinking coffee, but he went away when I came in."

"I'll go see," Paul said.

Flip waited, gnawing away on a chunk of bread and jam while Ariel tried to scramble onto her lap and share it with her.

Paul returned, saying, "Thérèse says there wasn't anybody there."

"There *was*," Flip persisted. "I saw him."

Paul sat down on the floor and helped himself to bread and jam. "Oh, well, he was probably one of Thérèse's boyfriends. She's always having her boyfriends in and feeding them things and then she pretends that they weren't there and she gave the food to Ariel. Just think, Flip, next Sunday you won't have to go back to school. You'll be living here."

Flip sighed, curled on the fur rug with Ariel licking her ear, and the warmth from the fire flickering over her body. "That will be wonderful. I can ski all day long and we can talk and talk and talk—" She had almost forgotten her disappointment at not being with her father.

The last day before the holidays really was as much fun as Erna and Jackie had told Flip it would be. The girls packed all morning and even Miss Tulip turned a deaf ear when they ran shouting up and down the corridor. Erna and Jackie chased Flip, who crashed into Madame Perceval at the head of the stairs and apologized abjectly, though her face was still flushed with pleasure and fun.

"Just a little more quietly, Flip," Madame Perceval said, but she smiled with satisfaction as she sent Flip running back to the others.

After lunch they were all sent out for a walk. Signorina took the walk and she didn't make them march in line but let them throw snowballs and tumble about in the snow. And she, too, smiled as she watched Flip gather up the snow in her scarlet mittens and hit Esmée Bodet square in the face. Of course Esmée spoiled it by pretending there was ice in the snow and trying to cry, but Signorina said briskly, "Now, Esmée, don't put on. You know you aren't hurt in the least. You just wish your aim were as good as Philippa's."

Esmée stuck out her lip and drew Gloria and Sally aside to read them her latest epistle from André, who was at school in Villeneuve.

After tea the term marks were read out in Assembly Hall. Flip was third for her class with Solvei Krogstad first, and Maggie Campbell second. Then there was a scramble to change for dinner, and when they got down to the dining room the huge fireplaces at either end were blazing and there was a big lighted Christmas tree in one of the bay windows. There was chicken for dinner, and all kinds of unaccustomed delicacies, and the tables were lit by candlelight, and Erna and Jackie called to Flip to come and sit with them so she didn't have to stand miserably around looking for a vacant seat as she used to do whenever there were unsupervised tables. All through the meal they sang Christmas carols in all languages. As each group started a carol of its country, the others would try to join in, sometimes just humming along with the tune, sometimes picking up the words of the chorus. And the big room was full of warmth and light and happiness and Flip wanted to push back her chair and go about the room and hug everybody.

If it could just be like this always, she thought.

After dinner the faculty gave their annual play. They had written it themselves and in it they were all inmates of an old ladies' home. They had chosen girls from the different classes to be matrons and maids. Liz Campbell, Maggie's sister and one of the older girls, was the nurse, and convulsed them all by telling Fräulein Hauser she was just pretending to have ·a sore throat to get out of her walk. Kaatje van Leyden with a black wool wig and a uniform borrowed from Miss Tulip was the matron and scolded Madame Perceval for not making her bed properly and having untidy drawers. The girls took off the teachers and the teachers took off the girls and the audience screamed with laughter during an all-too-brief half hour.

Then, while the actors got out of costume there was a wild game of musical chairs played by the entire school, from the youngest to the oldest. Flip astonished herself and everybody else by being left by the last chair with Gloria, who had got there by the simple method of pushing everybody else out of the way, but finally Flip sat down in triumph while Gloria sprawled, defeated, but grinning, on the floor.

Then the phonograph was turned off and Mlle. Desmoulins, the music teacher, took her place at the piano. They sang more Christmas carols and the school song, during which Martha Downs and Kaatje van Leyden went about quietly turning out all the lights until the room was lit only by the fire and the candles on either side of the piano.

Mlle. Desmoulins started playing *Auld Lang Syne* and *Gaudeamus Igitur,* and the girls all crossed their arms and joined hands, making three big circles, one within the other, and sang in gentler voices than they had used all evening. And it did not seem strange to Flip, standing between Erna and Solvei, that tears were streaming down Erna's cheeks and her mouth was trembling, so that she could scarcely sing, nor that there was a quaver in Solvei's usually steady voice.

As they were getting ready for bed Erna turned to

Flip and said with serious eyes, though her voice was bantering, "Flip, do something for me, will you?"

"Okay, what?"

"When you say your prayers tonight please pray that I won't have to go home for the spring holidays. I know they won't let me stay with Jackie, but please pray that I can at least stay at school."

"Okay, Erna," Flip said. "If that's what you want, I'll pray for it. But I'll pray that the holidays won't be as bad as you think they will, too, if you don't mind."

"It won't do any good," Erna said, "but go ahead and pray for it."

On the first day of the Christmas holidays Paul drove over with Monsieur Laurens to get Flip. He would not come into the school but waited outside, standing tall and straight beside the car, and as ready to flee as a mountain chamois. Most of Flip's classmates were standing with her in the hall, surrounded by coats and parcels and suitcases, and when they heard Monsieur Laurens tell Flip that Paul was outside they all made excuses to drift toward the window.

"What a dream boy," Flip heard Sally whisper to Esmée. "How did Flip ever get to know someone like that?"

"He must be younger than he looks," Esmée whispered back, and Flip repressed a grin.

Jackie and Erna came over to say good-bye to her. "Have wonderful hols, Flip," Erna said, shaking hands with her.

And Jackie squeezed her arm and whispered, "See you next year, Pill. Your Paul looks divine!"

Smiling and happy, Flip followed Monsieur Laurens to the car.

Paul took her up to her room in the gate house. It was a tiny cupboard of a place across the hall from Paul's room, painted a soft blue, with immaculate white curtains at the window. It was so small a room that the four-poster bed took up the entire space; there wasn't even space for a bureau or a chair, and Flip was given a carved sea-captain's chest in the hall in which to keep her things.

"And remember, don't close your door, Flip," Paul warned her. "The room's so small I guess you wouldn't want to, anyhow, but the latch is broken and you can't open the door from the inside."

"I'll remember," Flip promised.

As soon as Flip was unpacked she changed out of her uniform and into her ski clothes. Madame Perceval, who had stayed at the school until the majority of the girls were safely off on their various trains, had arrived, and they spent the day skiing. They took a funicular up the mountain and skied until dark, stopping at an inn for lunch. Then, at Flip's favorite time of day, when the sky was an intense green-blue and the bare branches of the trees were a delicate filigree against it and the first stars began to tremble above the mountain, they skied back to the gate house.

"Are you having a good time, Flip?" Paul asked anxiously. "Is everything all right?"

"It's wonderful!" Flip assured him. "I'm having a *beautiful* time."

After dinner she brought her sketch pad and pencil downstairs with her and sat in front of the fire, idly sketching Paul and Monsieur Laurens. Monsieur Laurens was easy, with his peaked eyebrows, his long thin nose, and his pipe, and his slippers run down at the heels, but she could not caricature Paul.

"Let me see," Paul said.

She showed him the pad. "I can't do you," she told him. "I can do your father, but I can't do you. I can't do Madame either. Why is it, Madame, that I can't do you and Paul?"

Madame Perceval did not answer the question. Instead she said, "Someday you must try a real portrait of Paul. I'll let you use my oils."

"Oh, would you, Madame!" Flip cried. "I'd love to try. Paul would make a wonderful portrait. Would you really sit for me, Paul?"

Paul grinned rather shyly. "If you'd like me to."

"Come on out in the kitchen," Madame said, "and we'll have a snack. And then it's time for you two to be in bed, holidays or no holidays."

After Flip was in bed, Paul crossed the hall and knocked on her open door.

"Hello," Flip whispered.

"Are you sleepy, Flip," Paul asked, "or shall we talk for a few minutes?"

"Come and talk."

Paul had his eiderdown quilt wrapped around him and he climbed up onto the foot of the bed and sat at her feet.

"You look like an Indian chief," Flip said, laughing.

Paul laughed, too, and then sighed. "I'm so glad you're here!"

"Me, too," Flip said.

She kneaded her feet against her hot water bottle and pulled her blankets up under her chin and the moonlight came in the window and the snowlight and the room seemed very bright and cold. She burrowed into the pillows and Paul wrapped his eiderdown tightly about him so that only his face and a lock of dark hair showed, and they giggled with pleasure at being there together, warm and comfortable and awake, with all the days and nights of the holidays stretching out before them.

"I'm hungry *again*," Paul whispered.

"I am, too," Flip whispered back.

"Are you hungry enough to do anything about it?"

"No."

"Me neither." Then, after a moment, Paul whispered, "Flip—"

"What?" she turned toward him, and gently his lips brushed against hers.

"I can talk about anything with you," Paul said, and again his lips touched hers. "I know you care about me, and that you understand how I feel about not—about not remembering."

The feel of Paul's lips still tingled against hers. "Some day you'll remember."

"Will I? The way you remember your mother?"

She put her hand lightly on the softness of the down quilt that covered his shoulders. "You know, Paul, you've made remembering my mother a good thing. I think of her, now, and it still hurts that I'll never see her again, but remembering is, well, it's a privilege. You've made me realize that."

"Tell me, then," Paul urged. "Tell me some more of the good things you remember. What was she like? Was she like Aunt Colette?"

Flip shook her head. "No. And—yes. I mean, they both make you feel you can be and do more than you think you can. And they both make you feel they can make everything be all right. Or at least bearable. They don't look a bit alike—Mother was very blond, but her hair was soft and curly, not a bit like mine, and her eyes were like women's eyes in Renoir paintings, soft and dark and tender. And she laughed a lot, and it sounded like spring. She told me lots of stories, and we read aloud together."

"Go on," Paul said. "Tell me something else. I think maybe, maybe hearing you tell about your mother might help me to remember. When you talk about her I get what feels like flickerings at the edges of my mind."

"Well—" Flip thought for a moment. "She really did have a way of turning things around and making them all right. Once when we were spending the summer with my grandmother in Goshen, one of the houses in the center of town burned. The sirens went off in the middle of the night. The firemen—they're all volunteers—got everybody out before anybody was hurt, and Mother took all the kids—there were four of them—home with us, and there they were in our kitchen, in their nightclothes, and Mother was feeding them sandwiches and cocoa, and making them all laugh, and they stayed with us, oh, for weeks, until they could get in their house again. I was little, maybe five, but I remember the way they all stopped being frightened the night of the fire just because Mother was there and they knew she'd make everything all right. They were alive, and their parents weren't hurt, and—" she stopped as Paul raised his hand.

Then he shook his head. "For a moment I thought I remembered . . . but it went away. Go on. Please."

"In the morning she used to come in to wake me, and her hair would be all around her, like a cape. Father painted her and painted her. She was about the only grown person he ever painted. He's never painted Eunice. Only sketches. I'll show you a picture of her tomorrow. Mother, I mean. And she took me to movies and plays and concerts and museums. On weekends and holidays we played together like two kids."

Paul did not respond, and Flip looked over the moonlight and there he was, sound asleep, his mouth a tiny bit open. She crawled out from under the covers and shook him gently. "Paul. Paul. You'd better wake up and go to bed."

He rolled over sleepily and slid off the bed, and stood there, clutching his eiderdown, and swaying as though he were still asleep. "Good night, Flip. Thank you." He bent down and kissed her again, then crossed the hall to his room.

Flip clambered back under the covers and put her feet against the warmth of the hot water bottle. She still felt the gentleness of his lips against hers as she slid into sleep.

A few days after the holidays began Flip and Paul were skiing alone. Madame Perceval had gone to spend the day with some friends in Ouchy, and Monsieur Laurens was deep into his book. Flip and Paul, their skis over their shoulders, had climbed a good distance up the mountain and were preparing to ski down when a voice behind them called, "Paul."

They turned around and Flip saw the dark man with the too-brilliant black eyes.

"Paul," he said again.

Paul stared at him blankly.

"Don't you know me?" he asked.

"No," Paul said.

"Alain, are you sure you don't know me?"

"What do you mean?" Paul said. "My name is Paul Laurens. What do you mean?"

"Your name is Alain." The man took a step toward them and Paul pushed Flip back a little. "Your name is Alain Berda. Are you sure you don't know me?"

"Why should I know you?" Paul demanded.

"Because I am your father, Alain," the man said.

For a minute Flip thought Paul was going to fall. All the color drained from his face and if he had not been holding on to Flip's arm, he could not have remained standing.

"No," he said. "No. You are not my father." And his voice came out as hoarse and strange as Flip's had on the morning she woke up with laryngitis.

"I know it's a surprise to you," the man said. "You are happy where you are and you don't want to remember the past. But surely you must remember your own father, Alain."

"You are not my father," Paul repeated firmly.

Now the man came a step closer and Flip felt as though she were going to be sick from distaste and loathing of him. She put her arm firmly about Paul. "If Paul says you aren't his father that's that. Good-bye."

The man smiled, and when he smiled, his face seemed even more frightening than when he was serious. "Perhaps you're thinking that I'm a shabby sort of person to be your father, Alain, but if I'm shabby it's because of the months and years I've spent searching for you."

"How did you find me?" Paul asked, and his voice was faint.

"I heard that a child answering to my lost son's description might be in a boarding school in Switzerland. You can imagine the months I've spent searching all the Swiss schools. I have spent hours watching the boys in the school up the mountain. I even looked at the girls' school down the mountain, hoping perhaps to come across someone who might have known you. That is when I first saw this young lady here." He nodded at Flip.

"Why did you tell me you were going to tend the furnace?" Flip asked.

"I couldn't very well tell you I was looking for a lost boy, could I? Then I saw Paul, as he is now called, and I knew that my search had come to an end. I've been watching you from a distance to make sure, but now there's no doubt in my mind that you're my son Alain." He opened his arms as though he expected Paul to run into them, but Paul clutched Flip even tighter.

"You are not my father," he said again, and Flip could feel him trembling all over. She herself was shaking and she felt very cold as she stood there in the snow with her arms about Paul.

"Go away!" Paul cried. "You're playing a horrible trick on me."

"I don't want to hurry you, Alain," the man said. "I know this must be a great shock to you. But remember that you have found not a stranger but a father who will love and protect you. Why don't you take me home to Monsieur Laurens and we'll talk it over with him?"

"No," Paul said. "You mustn't see my father."

"But why not, Alain?"

"My father is working. You mustn't disturb him."

"But about something so important, Alain?"

"No," Paul reiterated. "You mustn't see my father."

"Alain," the man said. "Suppose I could prove to you that I was your father?"

"How could you prove it? You're not my father. Stop calling me Alain."

"Alain," the man's voice was pleading. "Suppose I showed you a picture I have of you and me when you were little?"

After a moment Paul said, "Let me see the picture."

"It's up the mountain in the chalet where I'm staying. Come with me and I'll show it to you."

"No." Paul's voice was flat and colorless with shock and fear. "Bring it to me."

"Very well," the man said. "I'll bring it to your house this evening."

"No," Paul said again. "No. You can't go there. I'll meet you somewhere."

"Where?"

"Bring it to the château. Leave it there for me."

"I can't leave that picture lying around, Alain. It's all I've had of my son for a long time. But I'll bring it to the château tonight after dinner, at eight o'clock, and you can look at it and see if it helps you to remember."

"Very well. I'll be there," Paul said.

The man moved toward him as though to kiss him, but as Paul drew back in repulsion the man dropped his arms to his side and stood there looking at him. "I suppose it is too much to ask that you should know me all at once; but when we have lived together for a little while I am sure things will be different."

"Bring me the picture," Paul cried in a choking voice.

"Very well, Alain," the man said. "I will leave you now but I will see you at the château this evening." And he turned and started up the mountain and in a moment disappeared in a clump of trees.

When he was out of sight Paul bent down and fastened on his skis. His lips were pale and tightly closed and he did not say a word. Flip put on her skis and silently followed him down the mountain.

When they got to the gate house Paul said, "Don't tell my father."

"What are you going to do, Paul?"

"I don't know. But I know I can't tell my father."

"Why not?"

Paul's voice shook. "He might believe him. If my father believes him, I'll have to go with him."

"You don't remember him? You don't remember him at all, Paul?" Flip asked.

Paul shook his head.

"You don't think he is your father?" Flip asked.

Paul shook his head again and he was shivering.

"We'd better go in," Flip said. "You're cold."

Georges Laurens was shut up in his tiny study and Flip and Paul crouched in front of the fire.

"Thank goodness Aunt Colette isn't here," Paul said. "She'd guess something was the matter right away."

"I wish she *were* here!" Flip cried. "She'd know what to do."

But Paul shook his head again. "I know what I have to do."

"What, Paul?"

"I have to go to the château tonight and see that picture. Maybe that will help me to remember."

"You don't look like him," Flip said. "You don't look like him at all."

"No." Paul picked up the poker and jabbed miserably at the logs. "But you don't seem as if you look at all like either your mother or father, from their pictures."

"I don't," Flip said. "I look like my grandmother."

"Well, you see then? It doesn't mean anything if I don't look like him. But Flip, I'm sure if I saw my father I'd remember him. Don't you think I would?"

"I don't know," Flip said. "It seems to me you would."

Paul knocked all the logs out of place with the poker and had to take the tongs to put them back. "He's so hideous, Flip. Like a snake. Or a rat. And, Flip, if I were really his son and he'd spent all that time looking for me, it would be because he loved me, wouldn't it? And I didn't feel that he loved me at all. If only he'd had that picture with him. If only I could get it without going to the château to meet him tonight."

They sat looking into the fire. A log broke in half and fell, sending up a shower of sparks, and suddenly Flip thought of something that made a prickly feeling begin at the base of her spine and go all the way up her back. At last she said, "I know how you can get the picture without having to go to the château."

"How?" Paul asked eagerly.

"I'll go."

"Don't be a little idiot," Paul said. "As if I'd let you. Anyhow, he wouldn't give it to you."

"I could pretend I was you."

"I wouldn't let you."

"I could wear your ski clothes."

"They wouldn't fit you."

"They'd fit well enough," Flip said. "I'm not so much

shorter than you. And I could put my hair under your cap and in the dark he wouldn't be able to tell the difference."

Paul put his head down on his knees. "I won't let you do that."

"If you go," Flip said, "I'm afraid he'll never let you come back. He doesn't want me."

"Wouldn't you be afraid to go?"

"Yes," Flip admitted. "I would be. But I'd be more afraid to have you go than I would be to go myself."

"No," Paul said firmly. "It's wonderful of you to think of it. But it is impossible."

And Flip knew there was no use arguing with him.

Thérèse came in and stood arms akimbo in the doorway, announcing, "Lunch is on the table and it's good onion soup, so come and eat it while it's hot."

"I'm not hungry," Paul whispered.

"I'm not either," Flip whispered back. "But we've got to pretend we are. Does Ariel like onion soup?"

"Ariel likes anything."

"Well, that's all right then," Flip said.

A wind came up during the afternoon and by dinnertime it was howling about the gate house. Flip had thought up a scheme in which, in spite of Paul's opposition, she would be the one to make the trip to the château. But it was so daring, so dangerous, that whenever she thought of it she began to shiver. Her shivers started somewhere deep inside of her, the way she thought a tidal wave must start deep inside of the ocean, and then it seemed to break over her like a wave. Gloria said that when you shivered like that when you weren't cold it meant that somebody was walking over the place your grave was going to be.

They sat by the fire, Flip and Paul, huddled there all afternoon, scarcely saying a word, listening to the wind rise. Fortunately Georges Laurens was absorbed in his work and their silence did not penetrate his concentration any more than their conversation would have.

"If he'd just leave the picture for me," Paul said.

"He won't. He'll be there. He wants to make sure he gets you." Flip hugged Ariel for comfort.

After dinner they went upstairs and sat on Paul's bed.

"I'll go in five minutes," Paul said, staring unhappily down at the floor.

"Paul—" Flip started.

"What?"

"I want to give you something to take with you for good luck."

"I need good luck," Paul said.

"Well, in the old days a knight always carried the handkerchief of his lady. Would you like to carry my handkerchief?"

"Yes," Paul said.

"It's under my pillow. But it's a clean one."

"I'll get it and then I'll go." Paul got up and crossed the hall to Flip's room. She followed close at his heels and stood in the doorway, and when he had reached the head of the big bed and was feeling under her pillow for the handkerchief she slammed the door on him, the door that did not open from the inside.

"Flip! What are you doing!" Paul cried. "Open the door!"

"No," Flip called softly through the door. "I'm going to put on your ski clothes and go to the château." And she rushed into Paul's room and pulled on his brown ski trousers and red sweater, and pulled his striped stocking cap over her hair.

"Let me out! Flip, you devil! Let me out!" Paul cried, pounding against the door.

Flip took a hasty look at herself in the mirror as she pulled on Paul's mittens. I'll be all right in the dark, she told herself. "Good-bye, Paul," she called through the door to him. "I'll be back with the picture as fast as I possibly can."

Ignoring his frantic shouts, she hurried down the stairs. She was afraid that Georges Laurens would hear the commotion and come to investigate, but as she tip-toed past his study she saw that he was deep in con-centration, and Paul's cries were falling on deaf ears. Madame Perceval had taken Ariel with her, so she need not be afraid that the dog would arouse Monsieur Laurens or even Thérèse.

She let herself out of the house.

It was one of the coldest evenings of the winter and the wind slapped at her face like a cruel hand. Clouds were scudding across the moon and their shadows on the snow seemed alive and Flip kept jumping with fear as the shadows moved and made her think they belonged to some animate creature.

"He is not Paul's father, he is not Paul's father, please, God, make him not be Paul's father," she kept saying under her breath.

The château loomed up, a gaunt ruin. A night bird flew out of one of the windows with a cry that sent Flip's heart into her mouth, and various shutters and loose boards were banging in the vicious wind. She stood still on the snow for a long time before she dared to go on.

Then she almost ran, jumping sideways like a startled pony to avoid the shadows that moved so strangely across the white ground. Although she was expecting it, when she heard a whispered "Alain" her tense body jerked and she stopped stock still.

"Alain," the voice came again, and the man moved out from the shadows.

"Here I am," Flip whispered.

"It's cold," he said. "Are you warmly dressed?"

"Yes. Where is the picture?" She kept on whispering because that way the man was not as apt to realize that it was a girl's voice.

"Come with me and I'll give it to you."

"I want to see it now," Flip whispered.

"You couldn't see it in this light. It's up in my chalet just up the mountain. It's warm there and I'll have some nice hot soup for you."

"I've finished dinner," Flip whispered, "and I don't want to go to your chalet. I just want to see the picture."

"You still don't remember that I'm your father?" the man asked, and he stepped forward and took her wrist in his hand.

"No!" Flip cried, trying to pull away. "No! You promised I could see the picture! Let me go!"

"And so you shall see the picture, Alain, if you will come with me."

From one of the turrets of the château an owl cried, making them both jump, but the man did not loose his hold on her wrist. He took the bony fingers of his other hand and held her chin and turned her face up to the moonlight and said, "You mustn't be afraid of me, Alain, my boy," and then he shouted, "What kind of a trick is this? You're the girl!"

Before she knew what she was doing Flip had squirmed out of his grasp and was pelting across the snow, but he was after her and caught her with furious fingers. Flip screamed and fought, biting and clawing like a little wild beast, and the night was full of her screams and the man's snarls and the banging of boards and shutters and the cries of disturbed birds. Neither of them saw when a shutter was blown loose from a turret window and came flying down to strike Flip on the head. She dropped like a wounded bird to the snow and lay there motionless. She did not see the man staring at her limp body in horror, nor know when he picked her up and went into the château with her and dumped her there in the dark, a small inert bundle on the stone floor.

SIX
The Prisoner Freed

Flip was lying at the bottom of the ocean and all the weight of the sea was upon her, pressing her down into the white sands, and bells were ringing down at the bottom of the sea, ringing and ringing, and the tides came and went above her and the waves were wild in the wind and the breakers rolled and she lay with all the waters of the world pushing her down onto the floor of the sea and the bells rang and rang until finally they were dissolved into icy darkness.

She opened her eyes and she saw Paul's white face. She turned toward him and whispered weakly, "I didn't get the picture, Paul," and then she moaned because the movement of turning her head seemed to bring the waters of the ocean down on her once more. She tried to push the weight of the waters away from her, but her fingers closed on a handful of cobwebs. She felt that she was being lifted and then again she was drowned in darkness.

When the darkness finally rose it was a quiet and almost imperceptible happening. She felt the bright warmth of winter sunlight on her eyelids and she thought at first that it was a morning back at school and in a moment the bell would ring and she would have to get up. And then she remembered that now it was winter and it was dark until after breakfast and if she had been in bed at school the sun would not be warm against her closed eyes.

And then she remembered the night before, the man who said he was Paul's father, and she remembered the château and the picture, and the waters of darkness suddenly bearing down upon her, and she was afraid to open her eyes. Her lids still shut tight, she stirred faintly upon the pillow.

"You're all right, Flip. You're absolutely all right, darling."

Now she opened her eyes and there was Madame Perceval standing beside the bed saying, "Everything's all right, Flip. Everything's all right. Close your eyes and go to sleep, my darling."

So she closed her eyes and this time the waters were gentle and she felt that she was slowly drifting down a river of sleep and when she woke up she was no longer afraid to look.

She opened her eyes and she was lying in the big four-poster bed in the room in the gate house that Madame Perceval used; and Mlle. Duvoisine, not in her uniform but in a tweed skirt and the sweater she had been knitting the day of Flip's laryngitis, was sitting in a chair by the window, reading. As Flip moved, Mllc. Duvoisine rose and came quickly over to the bed. She put her fingers lightly against Flip's wrist and said, "Well, Philippa, how are you?"

"I guess I'm fine. Where's Paul, please? Is he all right? I couldn't get the picture!" Flip started to sit up in her anxiety, but as she tried to raise her head it felt as though a crushing weight were holding it down and a wave of nausea swept over her.

"You'd better lie still," Mlle. Duvoisine warned her. "You'll probably have that headache for a couple of days."

"Why? What happened?"

"A piece of one of the shutters blew off the château and gave you what your roommate, Gloria Browne, would call a bop on the bean." Mlle. Duvoisine smiled at her with a warmth Flip had never seen in her eyes before.

"Is Paul all right?"

"Yes," Mlle. Duvoisine assured her. "You can see him in a few minutes. You're a foolish little girl, Philippa. Did you know that?" But she didn't sound as though she thought Flip foolish at all.

"How did you get here, please?" Flip asked her.

"I came to look after you till Madame Perceval gets back from Montreux. I'm staying at the school chalet in Gstaad and I'm going back this evening since you're all right and won't need me any longer. Now if you're a good girl and promise to lie still and not get excited, I'll let Paul come in. He's been waiting at your door all morning."

"I'll lie still."

Flip lay very still while Mlle. Duvoisine was gone, but

she could not keep her heart from thumping with excitement. Paul opened the door and came in.

"Flip! Are you all right!"

"Paul! Are you all right!"

They spoke simultaneously and then they both laughed and Paul came over to the bed and kissed Flip and then stood looking down at her. Flip smiled up at him and strangely her eyes filled with tears.

"I thought he'd killed you," Paul said.

"No, I'm fine, Paul. Are you all right?"

"Yes, Flip. Yes, I'm all right and there's so much to tell you, only Mademoiselle Duvoisine from your school said that I mustn't excite you and of course she's right."

"You won't excite me. Please tell me."

Paul climbed up onto the foot of the bed and sat there, leaning his dark head back against one of the posts. His eyes were ringed with black and his face looked white and tired and as though he had not slept.

"Tell me, Paul, please," she asked gently.

"He's not my father." Paul closed his eyes and a look of relief came into his face. "He's not my father, Flip."

"He *couldn't* have been your father," Flip said. "Not that man."

Paul opened his eyes and tried to smile at her. "After you locked me up in your room I shouted and banged and my father—I mean Monsieur Laurens—never even noticed." Flip opened her eyes wide because it was the first time Paul had corrected himself when he called Monsieur Laurens his father. He continued. "He said he heard something, but he thought we were having some kind of a game with Ariel. He'd forgotten Aunt Colette had Ariel with her. Then Aunt Colette came home and let me out and I told her everything and we ran downstairs and roused Father and then we went to the château. Father took his gun. Sometimes he can be a very active man, Flip. It's only when he's writing that he seems to forget the world. We saw the man who said he was my father coming out of the château and Father captured him and the man told us a piece of shutter had struck you on the head and he thought it had killed you and he had put you in the château to protect you from the wind and he kept crying out that he did not want to be a murderer. And Aunt Colette and I rushed into the château and found you and—" Paul paused for a long time. Then he said, "I thought you were dead. But Aunt Colette said you weren't and then you said something and moaned and we carried you home and called the doctor and Mademoiselle Duvoisine from your school."

"Where's Madame?" Flip asked him.

"She's down in Montreux with the man who said he was my father. They're at the police station. You see, Flip, that's what he's been doing. I mean, it's his profession. He went around finding out about people who didn't know who they were and then he pretended he was related to them and got money from whoever had become their new families. Aunt Colette said he was ill and not right in his mind. He admitted that he wasn't my father, but it wouldn't have mattered if he hadn't, because when I saw you lying there all in a little heap inside the château in the dark and I thought you were dead, I remembered. I remembered who I was, Flip."

Flip lay very quietly on the bed. She didn't dare move, partly because it hurt her head to move, but mostly because it was another of those times when she knew it would be best for Paul if she was very still and very silent.

Paul put his head down so that his cheek pressed against Flip's feet and a lock of his dark hair fell across his forehead. "I'll try to be clear, Flip," he said, "but I want to say it as quickly as possible because it's a hard thing to say. My father was a writer. We lived in an old château—something like *our* château, Flip—that had always been in our family. During the war my father worked with the Maquis. He was the editor of one of the most important of the underground newspapers. I had an older sister, she was fifteen then, and she helped. So did my mother. Sometimes they let me run errands. Everybody helped who could possibly be used and sometimes I could do things without arousing suspicion that an older person couldn't do." He paused for a moment, and then went on. "One evening I was coming home after dark. I went in through one of the French windows. The room was dark and I stumbled over something. It was my sister. She was lying there just the same way you were lying in the château last night when I thought you were dead. I saw you lying there and you *were* my sister and it wasn't last night at all but the night my sister was shot. It was shortly after that that all of my father's work was uncovered and we were sent to a concentration camp. . . . I think if you don't mind very much I'll have to let Aunt Colette tell you the rest."

Again Flip wanted to say something that would give Paul comfort, but she knew that she was unable to. She lay there and felt the pressure of his cheek against her feet, until he lifted his head and stared up at her and his eyes were the gray of the lake and seemed to hold in their depths as much knowledge and suffering as the lake must have seen. He stared up at her and now Flip knew that she must say something. She pushed herself up very

slowly on one elbow, raised herself up and beyond the
pain that clamped about her head, and reached down
and gently touched Paul's dark hair. She suddenly felt
much older, and, unconsciously, she echoed Madame
Perceval's words. "It's all right, Paul. Everything's going
to be all right."

After a while Mlle. Duvoisine came back into the room
and sent Paul away and Flip slept again. When she
awoke Madame Perceval was in the room and she took
Flip into her arms and held her as her mother had held
her.

"You were very brave, little one," Madame told her.

Flip started to shake her head but stopped as the
abrupt movement sent the pain back again. "I wasn't
brave. I was scared. I was—I was like pulp I was so
scared, Madame."

"But you went on for Paul's sake, anyhow. That was
brave."

"Can you be brave and scared at the same time?" Flip
asked.

"That's the hardest and the biggest kind of braveness
there is."

"Oh," Flip said, and then, because the thought of
being brave somehow embarrassed her, she asked, "Madame, will this make me miss any skiing? I'm all right,
aren't I?"

"Yes, dear, you're fine. It's a miracle, but you didn't
have a concussion. You're just a bit bruised and bat-
tered. The doctor will look in on you again later this
evening, but he says you'll be up and about in a couple
of days and I'll work with you every minute the rest of

the holidays to make up for the time you'll miss. Now. Paul's asleep. Georges is writing and Mademoiselle Duvoisine's gone back to Gstaad. How about eating something? Chicken soup and a poached egg? Thérèse will be miserable if you don't eat. She blames herself for last night's episode and she was very upset about losing her new boyfriend."

"I'll eat," Flip promised. "Madame . . . Paul told me about himself . . . about having remembered . . ."

Madame Perceval looked at Flip gravely. "It will be better for him now, Flip," she said, "in spite of the pain of the memory. Before, he had lost his parents completely. Now he can never lose them again."

"And, Madame . . . there was more that Paul said you would tell me."

"All right," Madame Perceval said. "I'll just run down and get your tray from Thérèse first. I won't be long."

When Madame returned with Flip's tray she sat down beside the bed and said, "Mademoiselle Duvoisine thought I should wait till you were up to tell you about Paul, but he has already told you so much and he's anxious for you to know everything so that the knowledge won't be between you. I think you're strong enough to hear. But eat your supper first."

"Yes, Madame."

When Flip had finished Madame said very quietly, "Paul's parents were put into the gas chamber. He saw their bodies dumped with a pile of others afterward. The following month his little brother died in his arms. It happened not only to Paul, you must understand. It happened to thousands of other children."

After a long silence Flip said, "We don't know, do

we, Madame? We can't know. I mean none of us at school who haven't been through it. I thought it was awful when my mother was killed and they didn't tell me for a week and I couldn't understand why she didn't come to me, but it wasn't like that. And even Gloria losing her teeth in the blitz. She doesn't know."

"No, Flip. Gloria doesn't know."

"I feel it deep inside, Madame. But I don't *know*. How can you do anything to make up, Madame? How can you help?"

"Just never forget," Madame Perceval said. "Never take it for granted."

"I don't see how anyone *could* forget."

"It's far too easy," Madame Perceval told her. "But it's important for us to remember, so that we can try to keep it from happening again. That's one reason I'm not going back to school after Christmas."

"You're not going back!" Flip cried, and almost upset her tray.

"Steady," Madame Perceval said. "I hadn't meant to tell you so soon."

"Oh, Madame," Flip wailed. "*Why* aren't you coming back!"

Madame got up and walked over to the window, looking out at the fresh white world, swept clean by the wind the night before. "I feel that I've outlived my usefulness at the school. After the war when my aunt started it up again she needed me to help her, because she's not as young or as strong as she once was. But the school's reestablished now. Everything's running smoothly. I'm not really needed any longer. As a matter of fact"— Madame Perceval turned toward Flip with a half smile— "you're partly responsible for my leaving."

"Me? How! Why!" Flip cried.

"I think if I hadn't seen your father's letters with their drawings of forlorn and frightened children I might not have been quite so ready to accept when a friend I worked with during the war wrote and asked me to come and help her in a hostel for just such children. So that's where I'm going after the holidays, dear. It's on the border between Switzerland and Germany, right where I was during most of the war, so it will be good for me in many ways to make myself go there. Now, my Flip, I've talked to you far too long already. You're supposed to be resting. Mademoiselle Duvoisine will be angry with me if I've excited you."

"You haven't excited me," Flip said, and her voice was low and mournful. "Only I don't see how I'll bear it back at school if you aren't there."

"I'm surprised at you, Philippa." Madame Perceval spoke sharply. "I didn't expect to hear you talk that way again. I thought that was the old Philippa we'd left behind. Bear it! Of course you'll bear it! Things won't be any different without me than they were with me. I've never shown any favoritism at school and I never would."

"I didn't mean that!" Flip cried. "Madame, you know I didn't mean that! It just helps me if I know that you're there, and it's *because* you're so fair and—and just."

Madame Perceval took her hand quickly. "I apologize, dear. Please forgive me. I've been very unjust to you. I know you'd never expect favors of any kind. I should have been accusing myself, not you. I said that because I've been afraid that I might show how particularly you interested me—and I've always prided myself on complete impartiality. But you remind me so much of

Denise—my daughter. She died of pneumonia during the war. You look very much like her and she had your same intense, difficult nature and artistic talent. . . . I said we weren't going to talk anymore and I've been going a blue streak, haven't I? Take your nap and Paul will come in when you wake up. Mademoiselle Duvoisine and the doctor both say that security and happiness are the best medicine he can have, and you can give him a great deal of both. By the way, his real name was Paul Muret. It's nice that we can go on calling him Paul. Of course it's a common name, but Paul says he's always felt *right* being called Paul. It was my husband's name."

As Madame Perceval bent over her to put the covers around her, Flip reached up and caught her hand. "You're right to leave school and go to take care of the children at the hostel, Madame. I do know that. There may be some older ones like Paul."

During the remainder of the holidays Madame Perceval took Flip and Paul on skiing expeditions every day. Once they got on the train in the morning and traveled all day. Flip was beginning to feel more at ease on her skis than she was on her own feet. When she put on her skis her clumsiness seemed to roll off her like water and her stiff knee seemed to have the spring and strength that it never had when she tried to run in a relay race or on the basketball court or on the hockey field. Flip and Paul grew brown and rosy and the shadows slowly retreated from Paul's eyes and Flip looked as though she could be no relation to the unhappy girl who had moped about the school and been unable to make friends. Now when they met other young people on their skiing expeditions she could exchange shouts and laugh with them, safe in her new security of friendship with Paul, confidence in her skiing, and Madame Perceval's approval and friendship. She tried not to think that someone new would be taking the art teacher's place at school.

"By the way, Flip," Madame Perceval said once. "When the question comes up at school about the ski meet, don't mention my part in the surprise. Just say that it was Paul who taught you to ski."

"All right, Madame," Flip said, "if you think it would be better that way."

"I do." Madame Perceval looked after Paul, who had skied on ahead of them. "After all, the credit is really Paul's anyhow."

In the evenings after dinner they sang Christmas carols. Flip had taught them her favorite, *The Twelve Days of Christmas.* She had loved it when she was very small because it was such a long one, and when she was told that she could choose just one more song before bedtime, that would be it. So she loved it for its memories and now for its own charming tune and delicate words, from the first verse

On the first day of Christmas
My true love sent to me
A partridge in a pear tree . . .

to the twelfth verse when all the twelve gifts are sung with a glad shout.

On Christmas Eve Georges Laurens stirred himself from his books and they all went out and climbed up the mountain and brought home a beautiful Christmas tree. Flip and Paul had been making the decorations in the evenings after dinner, chains of brightly colored paper, strings of berries and small rolled balls of tinfoil, and Flip had carefully painted and pasted on cardboard twenty delicate angels with feathery wings and a stable scene with Mary and Joseph and the infant Jesus, the kings and shepherds and all the animals who gathered close to keep the baby warm. When the tree was trimmed they sang carols, ending up with *The Twelve Days of Christmas*. Paul took Flip's hand and threw back his head and sang.

> On the twelfth day of Christmas
> My true love sent to me
> Twelve drummers drumming
> Eleven pipers piping
> Ten lords a-leaping
> Nine ladies dancing
> Eight maids a-milking
> Seven swans a-swimming
> Six geese a-laying
> Five gold rings,
> Four calling birds
> Three french hens
> Two turtle doves,
> And a partridge in a pear tree!

On Christmas morning they sat in front of the fire and opened their presents. Paul saved his gift to Flip till the last and then held out the small square box shyly. Flip opened it and lifted out of pale blue cotton a tiny silver pear on a chain.

"I couldn't find any of the gifts from the carol," Paul said, "but this is a pear from the tree the partridge was in."

Flip looked up at Paul's eager face and her own was radiant. She wanted to say something to express her happiness but she couldn't, so she just flung her arms wide as though she wanted to embrace them all.

"Why, Miss Philippa," Georges Laurens said, "I never realized before what a little beauty you are. We should have Christmas every day!"

"Do you like the pear?" Paul asked.

Flip, her eyes shining, whispered, "More than anything."

Toward the end of the holidays Flip persuaded Paul to stop off at the school chalet one day when they were skiing at Gstaad. She felt that perhaps it wasn't very nice of her to want to show Paul off, but she couldn't help wanting it.

"The really nicest ones went home for the holiday, which is too bad," Flip told him. "Gloria's all right. Oh, and I think Maggie and Liz Campbell stayed and they're awfully nice. Maggie's in my class and she's always been polite and everything, not like some of the others, and Liz is two classes above. Jackie and Erna and Solvei are the ones you'll like best, though. You'll have to meet them when they come back."

"Erna's German, isn't she?" Paul asked.

"Yes," Flip answered quickly, "but Jackie Bernstein's father was in a German prison near Paris for six months until he escaped and Erna is Jackie's best friend. And you'll like Erna anyhow because she's going to be a doctor too."

"Well," Paul said, "let's get this business at Gstaad over with before we worry about anything else. The important thing is for you to get used to the snow conditions at Gstaad before the ski meet."

The trip to Gstaad went off very well. Flip was so preoccupied with putting Paul at ease that she forgot to be shy and awkward herself and astounded the girls by making jokes and keeping up a rapid stream of talk at the dinner table. And she and Paul kept having to remember that they mustn't talk about skiing, or let on that they weren't returning by train but had left their skis at the Gstaad station.

On the last night of the holidays Madame Perceval came up to say good night to them, and sat beside Paul on the foot of Flip's bed.

"It's good night and good-bye, my children," she said. "I leave on the five thirty-two, tomorrow morning, and Georges will take me to the train and be back before you're awake."

"Couldn't we see you off?" Flip begged.

"No, dear. I don't like leave-takings. And in any case it's best for you to be fresh and have had a good night's rest before you go back to school. Work hard on the skiing. Paul will help you on weekends, though you don't need much help anymore, and I expect to hear great things of that ski meet. So don't disappoint me. I know you won't."

"I'll try not to, Madame," Flip promised, and she knew that both she and Madame Perceval meant more than just the skiing and the ski meet.

"Paul," Madame said, "take care of your father and take care of Flip. I'll keep in touch with you both and maybe we can all meet during the spring holidays. Good night, my children. God bless you." And she bent down and kissed them good night and good-bye.

After the Christmas holidays, the exciting and wonderful holidays, there seemed to be a great difference in Flip and her feeling toward the school. As she ran up the marble staircase she no longer felt new and strange. She realized with a little shock that she was now an "old girl." Almost every face she saw was familiar and the few new ones belonged to new girls who had replaced her as the lonely and the strange one. She stopped at the desk where Miss Tulip was presiding as she had on the day when Flip first came to the school with her father and Eunice. Miss Tulip checked her name in the big register and handed her a letter. It was from her father.

"Oh, thanks, Miss Tulip," she cried, and slit it open.

"My darling Flippet," she read:

> I told you not to worry if you didn't hear from me for a week or so while I was traveling. I did get you off that one post card while I was in Paris having twenty-four hours of gaiety with Eunice and now I am in Freiburg in Germany and will be traveling about for a month or so around here and across the border in Switzerland. It seems a shame that I will be so close to you and not be able to come to you at once, but I missed so much time while I was in the hospital with that devilish jaundice that I must

work double time now to try to make up. However, I *think* I may be able to manage to be with you for your ski meet. I shall try very hard to make it. I want to see you ski (but, darling, don't worry if you don't win any prizes. The fact that you have really learned to ski is more than enough) and I want to see your Paul. I don't know where I shall be during your Easter holidays, but wherever it is I promise you that you will be there too and we'll sandwich in plenty of fun between sketches. And don't expect much in the way of correspondence from me for the next few months, my dearest. You'll know that I am thinking of you and loving you anyhow, but my work often makes me unhappy and tired and when I stop at night I fall into bed and it is a great comfort to me to know that you are warm and fed and well cared for and that you have learned to have fun and be happy. I know that it was difficult and I am very proud of my Flippet.

With the letter he enclosed several sketches and Flip thought that Madame Perceval would have liked them— except the ones he had done of his twenty-four hours in Paris with Eunice. Flip crumpled the Paris sketches up but put the others carefully in the envelope with the letter, slipped it into her blazer pocket and started up the marble stairs just as a new group of girls came into the hall and started registering with Miss Tulip.

On the landing she bumped into Signorina. "Have good holidays, Philippa?" the Italian teacher asked her.

"Oh, yes, thank you, Signorina, wonderful! Did you?"

"Lovely. But it is good to get back to our clean Switzerland. So we have lost our Madame Perceval. I shall miss her."

"Yes," Flip said. "Yes, Signorina."

Erna and Jackie came tearing up the stairs. "Hello, Signorina! Hello, Flip!"

"Pill, *mon choux*, it's good to see you!" Jackie cried as Signorina went on up the stairs. "When did you get here? Isn't it wonderful to be back?"

"Flip, *meine süsse!*" Erna shouted.

Perhaps it was not wonderful, but neither was it terrible.

A group of them congregated in the corridor, since Miss Tulip was downstairs and could not reprimand them. They all talked at once, laughing, shouting, telling each other about the holidays. Gloria could not wait to show them the black lace and silk pajamas Emile had sent her for New Year, nor to tell about Flip's visit to the school chalet with Paul.

"You should *see* Pill's boyfriend," she shouted, "you should just *see* him!"

"That child? We saw him," Esmée said in a disinterested voice.

"Out the window the day the hols began? Don't be a dreep, Es. He's no child. You're just jealous. Pill brought him to the chalet for lunch, and he's dreamy, positively dreamy, isn't he, Sal?"

Sally grinned and nodded. "He really is. I never thought Pill had it in her. She must have a whopper of a line after all."

"All I can say is hurrah for Flip," Maggie Campbell said. "I'd hate to see Esmée get her claws into someone as nice as that."

Esmée turned angrily toward the laughing Maggie but Jackie broke in. "I went to six plays and two operas. What did you do, Esmée?"

Esmée announced languidly, still with a baleful eye on Maggie, that she had gone out dancing every night and worn a strapless evening gown.

"Strapless evening gown, my foot," Jackie whispered inelegantly to Flip. "She'd look gruesome in a strapless evening gown."

Solvei had spent the holidays skiing with her parents. "I bet *I* could teach you to ski, Flip," she said.

Oh, horrors, Flip thought. What shall I do if she really wants to try?

Later that evening Erna pulled Jackie and Flip out of the common room and onto the icy balcony, whispering, "I have something to tell you, but it's a secret and you must promise never to tell a soul."

"Cross my heart and hope to die," Flip said, thrilled to be included in a secret that Erna was sharing with Jackie.

"*Jure et crâche,*" Jackie said, and spat over the balcony, imitating the tough boys on the city streets.

Erna was satisfied. "Well, it's something I learned during the holidays," she started. "Maybe you know it already, Flip. It's about Madame Perceval."

Jackie grabbed Erna's arm. "Don't tell me it's the story of Percy's past!" She almost shrieked.

Erna nodded. "You're *sure* you won't tell anybody?"

"I said *jure et crâche,* didn't I?" And Jackie spat over the balcony again. Unfortunately in her excitement she had not seen Miss Tulip walking below, and the matron jumped as a wet spray blew past her face.

"*Who* is up on the balcony!" she exclaimed.

"Please, it's only us, Miss Tulip," Jackie called down meekly.

"I might have known it," Miss Tulip said, craning her neck and looking up at them. "Naturally it would be Jacqueline Bernstein and Erna Weber. And *with* Philippa Hunter. I am sorry to see you keeping such bad company, Philippa. Get back indoors at once, girls, or you'll catch your deaths of cold, and you may each take a deportment mark."

They retired indoors, Erna sputtering, "The old hag! On the first day after the hols too. No one else would have given us a deportment mark."

But Jackie was giggling wildly. "I spit on her! I spit on Black and Midnight." Then she said seriously, "Percy would never have given us a deportment mark for that. I don't know how we'll ever get on without her. School won't be the same. Go on about what you were going to tell us about her, Erna."

"I can't in here. They'd see we were having a secret and all come bouncing about. We'll have to wait till Gloria goes to brush her teeth," Erna said, looking around as a girl with beautiful honey-colored hair curling all over her head opened the glass doors and came into the common room, glancing diffidently about her.

"Can you tell me——" she started.

Gloria, anxious to prove that *she* was an old girl, went dashing across the room to her. "Hello, are you a new girl? The seniors' sitting room is on the next floor, just over the common room."

"I'm Miss Redford, the new art teacher," the girl said, smiling warmly. "I was looking for someone by the name of Philippa Hunter."

"Oh. That's me. I mean I." Flip stepped forward and Gloria retired in confusion.

"Oh, hello, Philippa. Could I speak to you for a moment?"

Flip followed Miss Redford into the hall, and the teacher smiled at her disarmingly. "Madame Perceval wrote me that you were the best art student in the school and that you'd show me around the studio and give me a helping hand till I get settled. I feel terribly new and strange coming into the middle of things like this and this is my first job. I'm just out of the College of London and I'm afraid I shall make a terrible muddle of things."

She laughed, and Flip thought, Well, if someone *had* to take Madame's place, this one couldn't be nicer.

"Would you like to see the studio now?" she suggested. "I have about half an hour before the bell."

"I'd love to," Miss Redford said. "I've been up there poking around. It's really a wonderful studio for a school. I looked at some of your things and I see that Madame Perceval was right." She paused and panted, "I wonder if I shall ever get used to all these stairs!"

Flip was so used to the five flights of stairs that she never thought of them, but Miss Redford was quite winded by the time they reached the top.

"Of course my room is on the second floor, so I shall always be trotting up and down!" she gasped.

Much as Flip liked Miss Redford, she was glad the new art teacher was not to have Madame Perceval's rooms.

"Now, Philippa," Miss Redford said, "if you'll just show me where things are kept in the cupboards, I'll be tremendously grateful. I thought we might do some modeling this term, and maybe if any of the things are good enough, we'll have them fired. I found the clay, but I would like to know where everything else is kept."

Flip opened the cupboard doors and showed Miss Redford Madame Perceval's places for everything. She had just finished when the bell rang, and she said, "There's my bell, so I'll have to go downstairs or Miss Tulip will give me a tardy mark. I'm glad Madame Perceval thought I could help."

"You've been a great help," Miss Redford said warmly, "and if you don't mind, I'll probably call on you again. Good night, and thanks awfully."

❁

The others were in the room when Flip got downstairs. "Was I embarrassed!" Gloria exclaimed. "What did she want?"

"Oh, just to have me show her where Madame kept the things in the studio. Golly, I'm hungry. We always had something to eat before we went to bed during the hols."

"Honestly," Gloria said, "I think she might have let us know she was a teacher and not just come in like a new girl."

"She didn't have a uniform on," Jackie said reasonably.

"Well, lots of girls don't when they come. I think teachers should look like teachers." Gloria was not ready to be pacified.

"Percy didn't look like a teacher."

"Yes, but she didn't look like a girl either. What's she like, Pill, this Redburn or whatever her name is?"

"Redford," Flip said. "And she seemed awfully nice."

"If you think she's nice, she must be, you were so crazy about Percy."

"She said we were going to do things in clay," Flip said. "Aren't you going to go brush your teeth, Gloria?"

"I've brushed them."

"You have not," Erna cried. "You just this minute finished getting undressed."

"I brushed them before I got undressed."

"Oh, Glo, you fibber!" Jackie jumped up and down on her bed.

"You're just plain dirty," Erna said rudely but without malice.

"I am not!" Gloria started to get excited. "I did brush my teeth before I got undressed. So there!"

"All right, all right!" Jackie said hastily. "Don't get in a fuss. I'm going to go brush *my* teeth, though," and she looked meaningfully at Erna and Flip, who echoed her and followed her out into the corridor.

"I bet she hasn't brushed her teeth," Erna whispered. "She just knows I have something to tell you that I'm not going to tell her. My father said I wasn't to go around telling people, but you're so crazy about Percy, both of you, I thought it would be all right."

Miss Tulip bore down on them. "Girls! No talking in the corridors! What are you doing?"

"We're just going to brush our teeth, please, Miss Tulip."

"Go and brush them, then. I don't want to have to give you another deportment mark. Step, now."

"Yes, Miss Tulip."

"We'll meet in the classroom before breakfast," Erna whispered.

As she lay in bed that night, propped up on one elbow so that she could look down the mountainside to the lake, Flip had a surprising sense of homecoming. She had missed, without realizing that she had missed it, being able to see the lake and the mountains of France from her bed, and they seemed to welcome her back. And when she lay down, the familiar pattern of light on the ceiling was a reassuring sight. As she began to get sleepy she sang in her mind, "On the first day of Christmas my true love gave to me a partridge in a pear tree," and reached up to feel the silver pear on its slender chain around her neck.

"At last!" Erna said the next morning as the three of them slipped into the classroom.

"Go on, quick, before someone comes in." Jackie stepped onto the teacher's platform and climbed up onto the table, sitting on it cross-legged.

"Yes, do hurry," Flip begged, sitting on her desk.

"Well, I have to begin at the beginning and tell you how I found out."

"Is it tragic?" Jackie asked.

"Yes, it is, and Percy was a heroine."

"What did she do?"

"Stop asking questions and I'll tell you!" Erna exclaimed in exasperation. "First of all, I had perfectly wonderful holidays. I stayed most of the time with a nurse from the hospital. My mother and father are getting a divorce and I'm glad." And she stared at Flip and Jackie defiantly.

"Oh, Erna," Jackie cried.

"Well, Mutti's not a bit like your mother," Erna said,

"and she's never liked me. But my father was just wonderful and Marianne, she's the nurse, was awfully nice, too, and took me to the movies when she was off duty. And she told me my father was a great surgeon and a wonderful man and I saw an operation and I didn't faint or anything and my father told me he was very happy I was going to be a doctor and he'd help me all he could. And he talked to me lots and lots and said he was sorry he never had time to write me or anything but he loved me just the same and he'd try to write me more. And then he told me he and Mutti disagreed about many things and they disagreed about the world and Germany and people and things in general. They'd disagreed about the war and the Nazis, only father couldn't say anything because of my brothers and Mutti and me and everything. He said all the injured and wounded people needed to be taken care of and it wasn't their fault, mostly, not the fault of—what did he call them? the—the little people. So he felt all right taking care of them and he was glad I was here at school because he thought it was the best place in the world for me right now. And it was really wonderful, kids, because he'd always been kind of stern and everything and I'd never really known him before or felt that I had a father the way you two do, and now I have, even if Mutti still doesn't love me."

Flip and Jackie listened, neither of them looking at the other or at Erna because there was too much emotion in the room and they both felt full of too much pity for Erna even while she was telling them how happy she was. But they caught the sorrow in her voice when she spoke of her mother, and Flip felt that having your mother not love you would be the bitterest way of all to lose her.

"Well, I expect you're wondering what all this has to do with Percy," Erna continued, her voice suddenly brisk. "My father's brother, my Uncle Guenther, is a doctor, too, and he used to know Percy's sister, the singer, and he knew about this school and that's how I happened to come here. He was a Nazi for a while and then he wanted to stop being one and they put him in a prison, but they needed surgeons and so they let him out and he had to pretend he was a Nazi but all the time he was trying to work against them. Really he was. I know lots of them say that now because it's—what's the word father used—expedient—but Uncle Guenther really did try, and then he just took care of the hurt people like my father did because hurt people should be taken care of no matter who they are."

"It's all right," Jackie said. "We believe you. Do go on about Percy."

"Well, Percy's sister sang in Berlin for the Americans and Uncle Guenther came to see her and they got to talking about old times and everything and then they talked about the war and how it was awful that friends should be enemies and they each said they'd wanted to be on—on the side of life and not on the side of death. And Percy's sister said she hadn't been able to do anything but sing. Madame and her husband had been living in Paris where he taught history at the Sorbonne and Percy taught art at one of the *lycées*. They were both wonderful skiers and they left and came to Switzerland, to the border between Switzerland and Germany, and they became guides who helped people escape into Switzerland. Their daughter had died of pneumonia just at the beginning of the war and it made Percy very serious. Uncle Guenther said that before that she had been very gay and used to love to go to parties and things. Anyhow, they became these guides, I mean Madame and her husband did, and once when they were bringing a party over the border they were discovered and Percy's husband was shot just before they got into Switzerland."

Jackie's dark eyes were enormous, and Flip felt that it was difficult to breathe.

Erna continued. "Madame managed to pick him up and sling him over her shoulder and get him over the border, with shots ringing out all around them. When they were safe she set him down to see if he was still alive, and he was, but one of his arteries had been severed by a bullet, and he died, right there, while she was holding him."

"Oh, God," Jackie breathed.

"Uncle Guenther said they were really in love. He said he wouldn't mind dying that way, being held by the woman he loved, but it must have been hell for Percy."

"Oh, God," Jackie said again. "Her daughter and her husband . . ."

"No wonder we all felt something special about her," Erna said. "Uncle Guenther said she was a real heroine, and kept right on helping people get over the border. And she was shot once, but not badly, a bullet just grazed her thigh. Well, I just thought you'd want to know, and you were the only two people in school I could tell it to."

"We'll never say a word," Flip promised.

"Oh, Erna!" Jackie cried. "It's so awful! And it's like a movie, Percy going on helping people to escape and everything."

"It's going to be awful without her the rest of the year," Erna said. "I'm glad this Miss Redford seems nice."

"Thank you for telling me, too, Erna." Flip slid down from her desk as the breakfast gong began to ring.

"Oh, well, I knew you were crazy about Percy. Come on, time for food." And Erna hurried them out of the classroom.

The days really began to go by as Flip had never thought days at school could go. She remembered in the movies how the passage of time was often shown by the pages of a calendar being turned in rapid succession, and it seemed now that the days at school were being flipped by in just such a way. She would get up in the cold dark of early morning, dress, shivering, make her bed, and rush out to practice skiing.

"Where *do* you go every morning, Flip?" her roommates asked her.

"It's a secret," she finally had to tell them, "but I'll tell you as soon as I possibly can."

"What kind of a secret?"

"Well, I *think* it's going to be a nice secret," Flip said.

She spent Sundays skiing with Paul and usually stayed at the gate house for the evening meal.

"Flip, have you ever seen the others ski?" Paul asked her.

"No. Sometimes on walks we pass the beginners and you can see them from the windows of the gym. But the others usually take the train up to Saint Loup and I haven't seen them."

"Then you don't really know what you're up against?"

"No."

"So you can't really tell how you'll stand the day of the ski meet."

"No."

"Well—" Paul threw out his arms and pushed back his chair. "There's no use worrying about it. Aunt Colette said you should definitely sign up with the intermediates and she certainly ought to know."

There was a letter one day from her father. "I'm sketching at the hostel where your Madame Perceval is teaching," he wrote. "She's doing amazing work with the children here and they all adore her. She speaks affectionately of you and sends you her regards."

And Paul told her, "My father had a letter from Aunt Colette. She's met your father. What do you think about that?"

"It'd be nice if they could be friends," Flip said.

"Better than lustful Eunice?"

Flip shuddered. "I wish lustful Eunice would get out of the picture. Anyhow, Paul, they've just met, Father and Madame Perceval. It doesn't mean anything. I wish it did."

One Sunday while they were at the table Flip said to Paul, "Why don't you ski back down to school with me if your father will let us, and then I could sort of show you around and he could come and get you."

"No," Paul said.

"Why not?"

"I just don't want to."

"Why don't you go, Paul?" Georges Laurens put in. "It would do you good."

"Please, Paul," Flip begged. "School's been lots of fun since Christmas."

"You've certainly changed," Paul said, looking down at his plate.

"Yes, I have. And it's lots nicer. I'm not the most popular girl in school or anything, but they don't hate me anymore, and Erna and Jackie and Solvei and Maggie are nice to me and everybody likes it because I draw pictures of them. Anyhow, you don't have to come in or say a word to anybody if you don't want to, and you can go on avoiding institutions. But I want to ski back to school and I can't unless you go with me because I'm not allowed to be out alone."

"There you are," Paul said. "Rules again."

"Honestly!" Flip cried, and for the first time in speaking to Paul her voice held anger. "Prisons and concentration camps and things aren't the only place where you have rules! You have to have rules! Look at international law."

"You look at it," Paul said.

Flip was getting really furious. "All right, I will! And I'll see what happens when nations go against it! You have wars and then you have bombs and concentration camps and people being killed and everything horrible. You *have* to have *some* rules! Hospitals have rules and if you're going to be a doctor you'll be working in hospitals. It's just plain common sense to accept some rules! It's just plain courtesy! I never thought I'd see you being *stupid*, Paul Laurens! And if you're going to tell me you're afraid of a few girls, I won't believe you."

Paul stood up, knocking over his chair, and walked out of the room.

Flip sat down and she was trembling. She looked across the table at Georges Laurens, her eyes wide with dismay. "I've upset him. That was awful of me. I'm sorry."

"It's all right," Georges Laurens said. "Losing your temper that way was the best thing you could have done. Finish your tart."

Flip picked up her fork and began eating again, but now the tart that had looked so delectable when Thérèse put it in front of her was only something to be forced down. She had just swallowed the last bite when Paul came back and stood in the doorway.

"All right," he almost shouted at Flip. "Get your skis. Please come for me in an hour, papa."

"An hour it shall be," Georges Laurens said.

It took them less than half an hour to ski back to the school. Flip took Paul into the ski room while she put her skis in the rack. "I didn't mean to make you angry," she said. "I'm sorry, Paul. Please forgive me."

Paul shook his head. "No. You were quite right. Everything you said. I don't know what's the matter with me."

"Would you—" Flip asked tentatively, "would you mind if I brought Jackie and Erna down for just a minute? They're dying to meet you and it's—it's strictly against the rules."

Paul laughed. "All right. Go ahead."

Flip went tearing along the corridor and up the stairs. She slowed down when she came to the lounge because Fräulein Hauser was on duty, and walked as quickly as possible to the common room. Luckily Jackie and Erna were off in a corner together, reading a letter from Jackie's mother.

"Get permission from Hauser to go to the libe and

meet me in the room," she whispered. Then she hurried away and ran up the stairs, pulling off her ski jacket and sweater on the way. Jackie and Erna came in as she was throwing on her uniform.

"What's up?"

"Come on down to the ski room with me," Flip panted.

"Are you crazy?" Erna asked. "Hauser won't give us permission. The basement at this time of night is *streng verboten.*"

"Don't be a nut," Flip said, "Paul's down there. He came back with me. We can slip down the back stairs. Oh, come on, kids, do hurry."

Both Erna's and Jackie's faces lit up when Flip mentioned Paul and they followed her excitedly down the back stairs. For a moment when they got to the ski room Flip thought that Paul had run out on her, but, no, he turned to meet them with a grin.

"Hello," Paul said, pulling off his cap and bowing.

"Paul, this is Erna and Jackie," Flip said quickly. "Kids, this is Paul Laurens, Madame's nephew."

They all said hello and sat down on the benches.

Flip began to talk quickly. "Erna and Jackie are my roommates, Paul. You remember. I told you about them. I would have brought Gloria, you know, she's our other roommate—but she can't ever keep a secret. If you want anything spread all over school, you just take Gloria aside and tell it to her as a dead secret and you know everybody'll know about it in a couple of hours. She's lots of fun though. Oh, and you know what we did to her!"

"What?" Paul asked, rather taken aback by this jabbering Flip.

"The ears," Flip said to Erna and Jackie, and the three of them went off into gales of laughter. "You tell him, Jackie," Flip said.

"Well, Gloria *never* used to wash her ears," Jackie began, "so we wrote her a letter pretending it came from Signorina del Rossi—she's the teacher on our corridor. We didn't dare make it from the matron because she'd have given us deportment marks but Signorina's a good sport. Anyhow, Flip wrote the letter, and she imitated Signorina's handwriting, and it said that Gloria was to go to Signorina every morning right after breakfast for ear inspection. Black and Midnight—she's the matron and sleeps on our corridor too—inspects our fingernails every morning but she doesn't look at our ears. So Gloria got this letter and that evening we heard her washing and washing in her cubicle and the next morning we hid behind the door to the back stairs because that's opposite Signorina's room, and Gloria came and knocked on Signorina's door and we heard her tell Signorina she'd come for ear inspection. And Signorina was just wonderful. She never let on that she didn't know what it was all about but looked at Gloria's ears and told her they were very nice and as long as she kept them that way she needn't come back."

Paul laughed obligingly, then said, "It's time for me to meet my father now, but I'll see you all at the ski meet. It's pretty soon now, isn't it?"

Erna hugged herself in anticipation and said, "Fräulein Hauser told us at dinner that it was definitely going to be next Saturday. The lists go up on Friday, and it's tremendously exciting, signing up for things."

Paul gave a nudge. "I suppose you'll all be signing up for things."

"All except Flip," Erna said, and Paul gave Flip another nudge.

They said good-bye at the foot of the back stairs. Paul bowed gallantly and told Erna and Jackie how much he'd enjoyed meeting them.

"I'll be up in a couple of minutes," Flip said. "I just want to say good-bye and thank you to Monsieur Laurens."

When Erna and Jackie had gone, Paul put his hands firmly on Flip's shoulders and turned her around. Then his lips were against hers, his arms around her.

When he let her go, she was breathless, wordless.

He said, "I know we're still considered children, and that I have a lot of learning to do, and lots of years before I get through medical school. There are too many unexpected things that happen to people for me to ask you to make any promises, but I love you, Flip."

"I love you, too, Paul." She knew that he was right and that it was too early for promises and that many things could happen in the next years. But this was a memory that would always be a special treasure, and Paul had taught her about the privilege and the joy of memory.

They left the warm basement and the ski racks and the smell of wet snow and wool and warm wax, and went out to where Georges Laurens was waiting.

"Just a week more till the meet, Flip," Paul whispered.

"I know," Flip whispered back, and shivered, a child again.

"Don't be scared," Paul told her. "You'll be fine. But, Flip, how time has crept up on us!"

"Like the wolf at the door." Flip tried to laugh, then, her voice suddenly pleading, the voice of a very small, frightened girl, she begged, "You'll be there, Paul?"

"I promise," Paul said. "Don't worry, Flip. I'll be there."

Friday morning after breakfast the lists for the ski meet were on the board. Flip had rushed through breakfast as usual in order to get a last morning's workout on her skis, so she was the first to sign up. She took the pencil attached to the board by a long chain and looked at the intermediate events. There was form, which she signed up for; the short race, which she also signed for, though sprinting was not her strong point; and the long race, for which she had higher hopes. Then there was intermediate jumping, but she didn't sign for that. Madame Perceval had told her that she was good enough to jump without worry if ever there were a necessity or emergency, but the slight stiffness and weakness in her knee held her back more on the jumping than in anything else. So there was her name at the top of the intermediate lists, PHILIPPA HUNTER, 97, in careful, decisive lettering. She looked at her name and her stomach seemed to flop over inside of her.

But there isn't time to be scared, she thought. I'd better go out and ski.

When she came back in to get the mail the lists were pretty well filled up. Almost everybody in Flip's class was an intermediate. A few were in the beginners group and Solvei was an expert, but almost all the girls she knew best had signed under her name and none of them had failed to notice PHILIPPA HUNTER, 97, at the top of the list.

"But Flip, you don't ski!"

"Pill, did you know those lists were for the *ski* meet?"

"Flip, you didn't *mean* to sign up for the ski meet, did you?"

"Are you crazy, Philippa Hunter?"

She looked at their incredulous faces and suddenly she began to wonder if she really *could* ski. "Yes, I did mean to sign up," she told them.

"But Flip, you can't ski!"

"Fräulein Hauser said you couldn't learn!"

"She said she couldn't teach you!"

"Pill, you must have gone mad!"

"I'm not mad," Flip said, standing with her back against the bulletin board while the girls crowded around her. "I'm not mad. I did mean to sign." She tried to move away but they pushed her back against the board.

Fräulein Hauser came over and said, "Girls!" Then she looked at Flip and said, "Philippa Hunter, I want to speak to you."

The girls moved away and Flip followed Fräulein Hauser up the stairs. Now that Madame Perceval was no longer at the school Fräulein Hauser had taken her place as second to Mlle. Dragonet and most popular of the teachers. But Flip still stung from the gym teacher's scorn and when she drew Fräulein Hauser's table at meals she did not regard it as a piece of good fortune.

Now Fräulein Hauser led her to the deserted classroom and said, "What did you mean by signing up for three events in the ski meet?"

Flip looked stubbornly into Fräulein Hauser's determined, suntanned face. "I want to ski in them."

"Don't be ridiculous." Fräulein Hauser's voice was sharp and annoyance robbed her features of their usually pleasant expression. "You know you can't ski well enough to enter even the beginners' events, much less the intermediate."

"I've been practicing every morning after breakfast for an hour."

"I assure you, Philippa, that you are not a skier. You simply are not good at sports because of your bad knee and you might as well face it. You had better stick to your painting. I thought you were settling down nicely and I must say I don't understand this wild idea of yours in entering the ski meet. Now be a sensible girl and go downstairs and take your name off."

Now I shall have to explain, Flip thought, and started, "No, please, Fräulein Hauser, you see I really do want to enter the ski meet because—"

But Fräulein Hauser did not give her a chance to finish. "I'm sorry, Philippa. I haven't time to waste on this nonsense. Suppose you let me be the judge of whether or not you can ski well enough to enter the meet. Now go downstairs and cross your name off the list or I shall."

"But please, Fräulein Hauser—" Flip started.

Fräulein Hauser turned away without listening. "I'm sorry, Philippa," she said.

"But Fräulein Hauser, I *can* ski!" Flip cried after her. But the gym teacher was already out of the room and didn't hear.

Flip waited long enough to give Fräulein Hauser time to get to the faculty room. Then she walked swiftly down the corridor before she had time to lose her nerve, and knocked on the door to Mlle. Dragonet's sitting room.

When Mlle. Dragonet's voice called out "Come in," she didn't know whether she was filled with relief or regret. She opened the door and slipped inside, shut it, and stood with her back to it as she had stood against the bulletin board downstairs.

Mlle. Dragonet was drinking coffee and going over some papers at a table in front of the fire; she looked up and said kindly, "Well, Philippa, what can I do for you?"

"Please, Mademoiselle Dragonet," Flip said desperately, "isn't it entirely up to the girls whether or not we enter the ski meet and what we sign up for? I mean, Erna told me you didn't have to be in it if you didn't want to, and if you did, you could sign up for anything and it was entirely your own responsibility what you thought you were good enough for."

"Yes. That's right." Mlle. Dragonet nodded and poured herself some more coffee out of a silver coffeepot.

"Well, Fräulein Hauser says I must take my name off the lists."

"Why does she say that?" Mlle. Dragonet dropped a saccharin tablet into her coffee and poured some hot milk into it as though it were the one thing in the world she was thinking of at the moment.

"Well, when we first started skiing she said I couldn't learn to ski and she couldn't teach me and I had to give it up. Then Madame Perceval found out my skis were too long and there was a pair some girl had left that fitted me and Madame and Paul have been teaching me to ski. I've practiced every morning after breakfast for an hour and during the Christmas hols we skied all the time and went on overnight skiing trips and things and Madame said I should enter the ski meet as an intermediate. But now Fräulein Hauser says I have to take my name off the list because she doesn't know I can ski."

"Why didn't you explain to Fräulein Hauser?" Mlle. Dragonet asked.

"I tried to, but she wouldn't listen. I don't think she knew I had anything to explain. And Madame Perceval said I shouldn't say anything about her helping me. She said I should say it was just Paul, and I don't think that would have convinced Fräulein Hauser, no matter how good a skier Paul is, because I was so *awful* before. That's why I had to come to you, Mademoiselle."

Mlle. Dragonet picked up her pencil and twirled it. "So you've been keeping your skiing a secret?"

"Yes, Mademoiselle Dragonet."

"Whose idea was this?"

"Paul's. He thought it would be so much fun to surprise everybody."

"Was he coming to the ski meet?"

"Yes, Mademoiselle."

"I can see," Mlle. Dragonet said, "how Paul would think it was fun to surprise everybody, and how you would think it was fun too. But don't you think it's a little hard on Fräulein Hauser?" Her brown eyes looked mildly at Flip.

Flip countered with another question. "Don't you think Fräulein Hauser should have noticed that my skis were too long? I know she has so many beginners she can't pay too much attention to any one person, and I've always been bad at sports, but as soon as I got skis that were the right length for me I was better. I wasn't good, but at least it was possible for me to learn."

"And you think you have learned?"

"Yes, Mademoiselle. And it was Madame Perceval who said I should enter as an intermediate. I haven't seen the others ski, so I wouldn't have known in what group I belonged."

"So Madame Perceval taught you, did she?" Mlle. Dragonet asked. She put her pencil down and said, "Very well, Philippa. I'll speak to Fräulein Hauser and explain the situation. It's almost time for call over now. You'd better get downstairs."

"Thank you, Mademoiselle Dragonet. Thank you so much. And you won't say anything about its being Madame Perceval who found me the skis and helped me, please? Because she said it would be better not to, only I didn't think she'd mind if I told you under these—these —imperative circumstances."

Mlle. Dragonet smiled. "I won't say anything about her part in it. I promise."

"I'm sorry to have bothered you," Flip said. "I didn't want to, but I didn't know what else to do. I was desperate."

"It's what I'm here for, Philippa," Mlle. Dragonet said.

As Flip left Mlle. Dragonet's sitting room and started downstairs she wondered how she could ever live through the hours until the ski meet. The two months since the Christmas holidays had flown by like a swift bird, but the brief time until the next day stretched out ahead of her like an eternity.

Erna met her when she got downstairs. "You didn't get your mail, Flip. I took it for you."

"Oh, thanks ever so much," Flip said. "Oh, wonderful! It's a letter from father. Thanks lots, Erna."

There was just time to read the letter before call over if she hurried, and she was glad to escape the questions and exclamations of the girls who came clustering about her again, probing her about the ski meet, telling her that Fräulein Hauser had already crossed her name off the lists.

She ran down the corridor to the bathroom, locked herself in, and opened her father's letter. I'm so glad it came today, she thought. I need it to give me courage for tomorrow.

"My darling champion skier," the letter began.

How proud I am of the way you've worked at your skiing and I hope your triumph at the ski meet will be everything you and Paul could hope for. Now, please don't be disappointed, darling—as a matter of fact maybe you'll be relieved—but I don't think I'll be able to make it for the ski meet. You'll probably do much better if you're not worrying about my being there and the spring holidays will be here before we know it.

She sat staring at the closed white bathroom door in front of her, with the paint chipped off in places. She was filled with completely disproportionate disappointment. When she heard someone pounding on the door and calling, "Flip! Flip!" she could not keep the unwelcome tears from her eyes.

"Flip! Flip!"

She forced the tears back and opened the door and Erna and Jackie were anxiously waiting for her.

"Flip!" Erna cried. "You missed call over and Hauser's

simply furious and she wants to see you right away."

"She says you're sulking because she took your name off the ski lists. Oh, Flip, what *do* you want to be in the ski meet for anyhow when you can't ski!"

"I *can* ski," Flip said. "And I'm *not* sulking because of the ski meet. Father said he could come and now he can't." The tears began to trickle down her cheeks. "I haven't seen him since school began," she managed to whisper.

Erna patted her clumsily on the shoulder. "That's awful, Flip. That's an awful shame."

"Maybe he'll be able to come at the last minute," Jackie said. "Don't cry, Flip."

The door opened again and Fräulein Hauser, looking extremely annoyed, stood in the doorway.

"Really, Philippa Hunter!" she exclaimed. "I have seldom seen such a display of bad sportsmanship."

Flip drew herself up and suddenly she looked very tall and strong as she stood facing the gym teacher. "Fräulein Hauser," she said. "I did not skip call over because you took my name off the ski lists. I didn't even know you'd taken it off. I am crying because I expected to see my father and now I'm not going to."

Fräulein Hauser looked at the tear-blurred face and the crumpled letter and at Erna and Jackie nodding in corroboration of Flip's words and said, more gently, "I'm sorry I misunderstood you, Philippa." And she smiled. "But you can hardly blame me."

"Please, Fräulein Hauser," Flip said. "I've been trying to tell you that I did learn to ski."

"Philippa, we settled that question this morning. Let's not reopen it." Fräulein Hauser's voice was short again.

"Get along to your classroom, and quickly, all three of you. It's almost time for the bell."

At lunchtime Flip's name was written in again over the heavy red line Fräulein Hauser had used to cross it out.

"Flip, you didn't put your name back!" Erna cried.

Flip shook her head desperately. "I didn't! It's not my writing! It's Fräulein Hauser's writing! Mademoiselle Dragonet gave me permission to be in the ski meet. Paul taught me how to ski." She put her hands to her head. "If I'd thought there'd be all this fuss and bother I'd never have entered the old ski meet!" Her head was a wild confusion of misery.

If I could just tell them it was Madame who taught me how to ski, that would make it all right, she thought.

"Hey, Flip," Erna said. "If you don't want your pudding, I do."

After lunch Kaatje van Leyden sought her out. "Look here, Philippa, I hear you're entering the ski meet."

Flip looked up at the older girl. "Yes, Kaatje."

"Fräulein Hauser says you can't ski."

"If I couldn't ski, I wouldn't have entered the ski meet," Flip said. Her mind was beginning to feel cold and numb the way her hands did in the very cold mornings when she was out skiing.

"Did you know that the points made or lost in the ski meet count for the school teams?" Kaatje asked. "You could make a team lose for the year if you pulled it down badly enough in the ski meet."

"I won't pull it down," Flip said, but she was beginning to lose faith in herself.

"Which team are you?"

"Odds. I'm number ninety-seven. Please, Kaatje. I promise you I can ski. I know I've pulled the Odds down in my gym work but I won't pull them down in the ski meet."

"But how did you learn to ski? Fräulein Hauser said you were so helpless she couldn't teach you. Sorry, but that's what she said and the ski meet's tomorrow so there isn't time to beat around bushes."

"Please, Kaatje," Flip said, "Paul Laurens, Madame Perceval's nephew, taught me every weekend, and he's a wonderful skier, and we skied during the holidays all the time and I've practiced an hour every morning after breakfast. Please, Kaatje, please, believe me!" Flip implored.

Kaatje put her hands on her hips and looked at Flip. "I don't know what to think. I'm captain of the Evens as well as school games captain and if the Evens win through your losing points, the Odds are going to blame me for it."

"Do you think Mademoiselle Dragonet would have put my name back on the lists if she'd thought I couldn't ski?"

"That's just it," Kaatje said. "I wouldn't think so, but you never know what the Dragon's going to take it into her head to do. If she's given you permission and you insist that you can ski I suppose there's nothing I can do about it." Then her frown disappeared and she gave Flip a friendly grin. "Here's good luck on it anyhow," she said, holding out her hand.

"Thanks, Kaatje," Flip said, taking it.

It couldn't have been a better day for a ski meet. It was very cold and still and the sky was that wonderful blue that seems to go up, up, up, and the sun seemed very bright and very far away in the heavens. The snow sparkled with blinding brilliance and everybody was filled with excitement.

But Flip sat in the train on the way up to Gstaad and she felt as cold and white as the snow and not in the least sparkling. Paul left Georges Laurens with Mlle. Dragonet and Signorina del Rossi and came and sat next to Flip. Erna and Jackie and the others greeted him with pleased excitement. Flip heard Sally whispering to Esmée, "Didn't I tell you he was divine?"

"So you taught Flip to ski!" Solvei exclaimed.

"I didn't have to do much teaching," Paul said. "She's a born skier."

Esmée got up from her seat and stood by them, attracted to the male presence like the proverbial fly to honey. "I'm just dying to see Flip ski," she said, smiling provocatively at Paul. "You were just wonderful to teach her."

"Esmée, sit down," Miss Armstrong called from the end of the car, and Esmée reluctantly withdrew.

Flip stared out the window with a set face. Her cheeks felt burning hot and her hands felt icy cold and she had a dull pain in her stomach. I'm sick, she thought. I feel awful. I should have gone to Mlle. Duvoisine and she'd have taken my temperature and put me in the infirmary and I wouldn't have had to be in the ski meet.

But she realized that the horrible feeling wasn't because she was ill, but because she was frightened. She was even more frightened than she had been the night she went to the château to meet the man who said he was Paul's father.

She was hardly aware when Paul left her to join the spectators, or when Erna pushed her into place to wait until the beginners had finished. Flip watched the beginners carefully and took heart. She was much more steady on her skis, they were much more a part of her, than they were on any of the girls in the beginners group, and she knew that she executed her turns with far more precision and surety than any of them. She looked at the beginners and she looked at the judges—Fräulein Hauser, and Miss Redford, who had turned out to be quite an expert skier, from the school; a jolly-looking Englishwoman who was sportsmistress at the English school down the mountain; and two professional skiers who sat smiling tolerantly at the efforts of the beginners.

After the beginners had been tested for form they had a short race which was won by little Lischen Bechman, one of the smallest girls in the school, and then Flip felt Erna pushing her forward. She stood in line with all the rest of the intermediates, between Erna and Maggie Campbell. One of the professional skiers stood up to give the directions. Flip snapped on her skis and pushed off with the others. She followed directions in a haze and was immeasurably grateful for the hours of practice which made her execute her Christianias and telemarks with automatic perfection. The judge told half the girls to drop out, but Flip was among those left standing as the judge put them through their paces again.

Now all but five of the girls were sent to the side, Flip, Erna, Esmée Bodet, Maggie Campbell, and Bianca Colantuono. Flip's mouth felt very dry and the tip of her tongue stuck out between her teeth. This time the judge only kept them a few minutes.

Jumping was next and only a few of the intermediates had entered that. Girls clustered around Flip, exclaiming, laughing, "Why, Flip, you old fox, you!"

"Why did you keep this up your sleeve, Pill?"

"Did Hauser *really* refuse to teach you?"

And Kaatje van Leyden came over from the seniors and shook her hand, saying, "Good work, Philippa. You really knew what you were talking about, didn't you? The Odds don't have to worry about *your* being on their team."

Flip blushed with pleasure and looked down at the snow under her feet and she loved it so and was filled with such excitement and triumph that she wanted to get down on her knees and kiss it, but instead she watched the jumpers. She felt that Erna was by far the best and was pleased with the thought that she would win.

Then it was time for the short race. Flip stood poised at the top of the hill and launched herself forward at the signal. She tried to cut through the cold air with the swift precision of an arrow and was pleased when she came in fifth, because Madame had told her not to worry about the short race, to enter it only for experience, because she would do best in the long race.

While the seniors lined up for form, Flip and the other intermediates who had signed up for the long race got on the funicular to go up to the starting point farther up the mountain. Madame Perceval had taken Flip over the course of the race several times during the holidays so she was almost as familiar with it as the other girls who had been skiing it once a week with Fräulein Hauser.

They were all tense as they lined up at the starting point. Kaatje van Leyden gave the signal and they were off. Flip felt a sense of wild exhilaration as she started down the mountain, and she knew that nothing else was like this. Flying in a plane could not give you this feeling of being the bird, of belief in your own personal wings.

Before the race was half over it became evident that it was to be between Flip, Erna, and Esmée. Flip's mind seemed to be cut cleanly in half; one half was filled with pure pleasure at the skiing and the other with a set determination to win this race. The three of them kept very close together, first one, then another, taking the advantage. Then, as they had to go through a clump of trees, Erna took the lead and pushed ahead with Flip next and Esmée dropping well behind.

Flip made a desperate effort and had just spurted ahead of Erna when she heard a cry, and, looking back, she saw Erna lying in the snow. She checked her speed, turned, and went back. As Erna saw her coming she called out, "Go on, Flip! Go on! Don't worry about me!"

But she ended on a groan and Flip continued back up the mountainside. Esmée flashed by without even looking at Erna, and Flip, as she slowly made her way up the snow, thought, I've lost the race.

But she knelt by Erna and said, "What happened?"

"Caught the tip of my ski on a piece of ice," Erna gasped. Her face was very white and her lips were blue with pain and cold. "You shouldn't have come back."

"Don't be silly," Flip said, and her voice sounded angry. "Is it your ankle?"

"Yes. I think I've busted it or something."

Flip unstrapped Erna's skis and took them off. "It may not be broken. It may be a sprain."

Erna's lips were white. "It hurts."

"What's up?" Kaatje van Leyden, who had been skiing down the mountainside with them, drew up beside them.

"Erna's hurt her ankle," Flip said. "I don't want to take off her boot because it will keep the swelling down. But she certainly can't ski."

Now more of the racers came in sight, but Kaatje waved them on. "Esmée's won but we might as well see who comes in second and third."

"Flip lost the race because of me," Erna told Kaatje. "She was way ahead of Esmée but when I fell she turned around and came back to me."

"And Esmée went on?" Kaatje asked.

"Sure Esmée went on," Erna said. "Esmée's Esmée. And Flip's Flip."

"Good for you, Philippa," Kaatje said. "Hurt badly, Erna?"

Erna, her teeth clenched, nodded.

"Philippa, if we make a chair with our hands do you think we can ski down together with Erna? It will be quite a job not to jolt her, but I think we'd better get her down to Duvoisine as soon as possible. How about it?" Kaatje asked.

"Okay," Flip said.

Jackie, trailing gallantly down at the tail of the race, stopped in dismay at the sight of Erna lying on the ground and helped her up onto Flip's and Kaatje's hands. Then they started slowly down the mountain. This was the most difficult skiing Flip had ever done, because she did not have her arms to help her balance herself and she and Kaatje had to ski as though they were one, making their turns and swerves in complete unison in order not to jolt Erna, who was trying bravely not to cry out in pain. Jackie had skied on ahead and Mlle. Duvoisine was waiting for them with the doctor, and Erna was borne off to the chalet to be administered to. Flip looked almost as limp and white as Erna as she went to join the other intermediates who were eating sandwiches while they waited for the expert events to be finished.

So now it was all over. She thought she had done well in form, but she had lost both races. She felt too tired, and too depressed now that her part in the long-waited-for meet was over, to be elated simply because she had skied well.

Just as Kaatje van Leyden came swooping down to win the long race, Jackie said, "Here's Erna," and Mlle. Duvoisine was pushing Erna, sitting on one chair, her bandaged foot in a green ski sock with a large hole in the toe, on another, across the snow to them. They all clustered about her.

"How are you, Erna?"

"Is it broken?"

"Does it hurt?"

"I'm fine," Erna told them as Mlle. Duvoisine left her with them. "It's just a sprain. It hurts like blazes and I have to go to the infirmary when we get back to school but Duvoisine says I can stay for the prizes. Kaatje's up talking to the judges. They must be ready to begin. Give me a sandwich, somebody, quick."

Fräulein Hauser stood up in the judges' box and blew her whistle. On the table in front of her was a box with medals and the silver cup. Everybody stopped talking and waited.

"I want to say that I am proud of the way you all skied today," Fräulein Hauser told them. "I think that you put on a splendid and professional showing. . . ."

As Fräulein Hauser continued, Flip began to look around at the spectators, and suddenly she saw her father. He did come! she thought happily. He did manage to get here even if I didn't win anything.

Then she saw that he was standing beside a woman, and that the woman had her hand plunged into his pocket to keep warm, in an intimate gesture.

Not Eunice.

Colette Perceval.

"And now," Fräulein Hauser was saying, "I have a pleasant surprise for all of you. An old friend has consented to give out the awards, someone I know you will all be delighted to see. Suppose I let her speak for herself."

Colette Perceval took her hand out of Philip Hunter's pocket and walked across the snow and climbed the steps to the judges' box as a cheer of welcome came from the girls.

"Percy!"

"Madame Perceval!"

"But I didn't *see* her!"

"Who's that man she's with?"

"Percy! How super!"

Everyone was whispering in low and excited whispers. Then Madame Perceval held up her hand and there was silence. Flip was so dazzled and delighted that she missed Madame Perceval's first words, though she was vaguely aware of the girls laughing and applauding. Then she tried to listen.

"And now for the awards," Madame Perceval was saying. "I won't delay that exciting information a moment longer. I'm afraid my train was late so I didn't see any of the beginners' events, but I hear from all the judges that none of you can be called beginners anymore, and the three of you who have won medals have every right to be proud of yourselves."

I won't win anything, Flip thought, as Madame Perceval gave out the medals, and Paul will be disappointed and Madame will think I didn't work . . .

"The judges feel unable to award a medal for Form to the intermediates as there was nothing to choose from between Margaret Campbell, Philippa Hunter, and Erna Weber. But each of these girls will be given a Certificate of Merit. The medal for Intermediate Jumping goes to Erna Weber, who is at the moment a fallen hero on the field of battle. Erna, will you send someone up for your medal, please?"

Erna gave Jackie a shove.

"The medal for the Short Race goes to Esmée Bodet, with certificates to Margaret Campbell, second, and Bianca Colantuono, third. Esmée Bodet seems to be the speed demon of the intermediates; the medal for the Long Race goes to her, too. . . ."

Now Flip began to look around at the spectators, and she saw her father standing between Paul and Monsieur Laurens, and her joy at seeing him was so great that it was like an ache.

"Hey, Flip." Jackie gave her a poke. "Percy's giving out the cup. Listen."

Again Flip had missed half of Madame's words, but she turned away from her father and looked up at the speaker's platform.

"This cup stands for more than just excellence in skiing or marked improvement," Madame Perceval was saying, "and I am happy that the judges were unanimous in their decision as to the girl who deserves it. I don't think there's any question in anybody's mind that this girl's improvement in skiing has been almost spectacular. But I think that you would all like to know that she lost a very good chance to win the long race by turning back to help a friend who had hurt herself, and then helped Kaatje van Leyden carry her down the mountain, a very difficult piece of skiing. The judges, especially those of us from the school who have watched her all winter, feel that she has tried harder, and accomplished more, than any other girl in school." Madame Perceval paused for a moment, then she said, "It gives me great pleasure to award this cup to Philippa Hunter."

Erna and Jackie pushed her forward and all her long-legged clumsiness returned to her as she crossed the blazing expanse of snow between the girls'and the judges' box. She tripped over a boot lace, fell to her knees, and got up, grinning, as everybody laughed and clapped. When Madame Perceval handed her the cup and stood there smiling down at her the storm of applause was so deafening that she knew they were glad she had won this most desired of all the awards, and that the applause was an honor as great as the cup itself. All the judges shook hands with her, and Fräulein Hauser said, rather awkwardly, "I seem to have made a big mistake, Philippa. I'm very glad."

Then the girls came clustering about her, shouting, "Well done, Flip! Good old Pill! Good for you, Philippa!" And she was laughing and blushing and stammering until she was swept off her feet and her father's arms were around her and he was exclaiming, "I'm proud of my girl!"

"Oh, father!" she cried. "You *did* come!"

"I managed to get away at the last minute," he told her. "So Colette—Madame Perceval—and I came over together."

Then Flip felt herself caught in someone else's arms and Madame Perceval kissed her on both cheeks. "I knew you'd make us proud of you, my darling," she cried.

"Oh, Madame!" Flip said, and all she seemed to be able to say was "Oh."

❋

She sat that night in front of the fire in the lodge, leaning back, her head against her father's knee, and watched the flames roar up the chimney, and a deep feeling of contentment like the warmth from the fire filled her whole body.

Earlier that evening, when they had been alone for a few minutes, Flip had asked her father, "What about Eunice?"

"What *what* about Eunice?" he had asked, smiling.

With courage she had not possessed when she had said good-bye to him at the beginning of school, she asked, "Is she still lusting after you?"

Philip Hunter threw back his head and laughed. "Poor Eunice. She's not that bad, Flippet, and she meant to be kind to you, truly she did."

"Yes, but what about her?" Flip prodded.

"Were you afraid I was getting serious about her?"

"She was certainly getting serious about you."

"No, Flippet." He tousled her hair. "I made it very clear to Eunice that I was in no way ready to be serious about anybody. It takes a man a long time to recover from the death of a wife. I loved your mother very much, as you know, and it wouldn't have been fair to Eunice to let her think I was ready to love again. But you're right, in a way. She did want more from me than I could give her, and we've said good-bye."

"What about Madame Perceval?" Flip asked, while she was still feeling brave.

"I don't think Colette is lusting after me, if that's what you're driving at." The crinkles at the outside of his eyes moved upwards in amusement.

"No, that's not what I'm driving at."

"What, then?"

Now Flip returned his smile. "If you want to lust after her it's all right with me."

Philip Hunter put his arm around her and hugged her. "Bless you, my Flip. Colette and I are good friends. I hope we will be good friends forever. We have much in common, including grief. But it's only a little over a year since your mother's death. I need more healing time, and Colette understands that. But we are friends."

"I'm glad," she said.

His arm tightened around her. "And I'm glad you're glad."

Dinner that evening at the lodge was a merry one, with lots of laughter. Paul was as relaxed as Flip had ever seen him, joining in the fun and even telling a joke. After dinner he sat on the hearthrug by Flip, pulling patient Ariel's ear. Colette Perceval sat companionably on the sofa next to Philip Hunter. Monsieur Laurens had retreated into his study after dinner.

"I'm so happy," Flip said, "that I haven't room for one

drop more. One drop more and I'll burst." She leaned back against her father's knees. Her body felt heavy and tired and comfortable and her stomach was full of Thérèse's onion soup.

"Remember how you were going to be the prisoner of Chillon, Flippet?" her father asked.

"I remember," she said, and smiled because she felt so free, and she knew that the freedom was in herself, just as the prison had been. She stood up and said, "I'll be back in a minute," because the happiness in her chest had grown to such proportions that she knew she had to go outside and let some of it escape into the night.

She pulled her coat off the peg in the hall and pushed into it, pulling up the hood as she opened the door and slipped outside. She looked down the mountainside to the lake, and across the lake to the mountains, and above the mountains to the stars. The night was all about her, wild and cold and beautiful, and she let her happiness spread out into it, so that it became part of the night, part of the lake and the mountains and the stars.

Then she turned and Paul was shutting the door and crossing the snow to stand beside her.

"I thought we should leave them alone—your father and Aunt Colette."

Flip reached for his hand. "They're good friends. That's enough for now."

Paul leaned toward her, kissing her gently. "And this is enough for now. For now," he repeated, and kissed her again. Then, "Let's go for a walk."

Still holding his hand, tightly, she said, "Yes, Paul."

"Let's walk over to the château," he suggested. "It's— it's sort of our place. You risked your life for me there . . ."

"And Ariel brought me to you there . . ."

"Oh, Ariel!" he cried, and ran back to the lodge and opened the door, whistling. Ariel came bounding out, barking, until Paul commanded him to be quiet.

They walked along quietly, hand in hand. Philippa and Paul.

It was not an ending. It was a beginning.

About the Author

MADELEINE L'ENGLE is the author of numerous books, among them the Newbery Award–winning *A Wrinkle in Time*; *A Wind in the Door*; and *A Swiftly Tilting Planet*. Her novel *A Ring of Endless Light* was named a Newbery Honor Book; it is the third volume of the Austin Family Trilogy, the other two of which are *Meet the Austins* and *The Moon by Night*. Her other books include *Camilla, Dragons in the Waters, The Young Unicorns*, and *The Arm of the Starfish*. Madeleine L'Engle lives in New York City with her husband.